MW00569457

Creaking in their Skins

For Eric,

On the occasion of
his last birthday
in the 20th Century,

Love,

Steve, May,
& Cemi

Other Collections of Short Stories from Quarry Press

Creaking in their Skins

■ ■ ■

MICHAEL WINTER

Quarry Press

The author would like to thank the following institutions for their support:
The Canada Council, Newfoundland & Labrador Arts Council, Banff
Centre for the Arts, and St. John's City Arts Jury.

Some of these stories have appeared in a different form in *The Malahat
Review*, *The Capilano Review*, *The New Quarterly*, *Canadian Author &
Bookman*, *Canadian Fiction Magazine*, *West Coast Line*, *Event*, and *Prairie
Fire*. "Two Families" won the 1993 Newfoundland Arts & Letters
Competition. It was printed, along with a version of "Creaking in their
Skins," in *Extremities: Fiction from the Burning Rock* (Killick Press 1994), a
collection of Newfoundland fiction.

The author is indebted to the following for their love, laughter, criticism
and afterglow: Larry Mathews, Lisa Moore, Claire Wilkshire, Stephanie
Squires, and the remaining embers of the Burning Rock Collective.
Thanks to Jane and Edna, mainland embers with no less a residual spark.
And of course the Blatchites on Cannery Row.

The publisher gratefully acknowledges the support of The Canada
Council, the Ontario Arts Council, the Department of Canadian Heritage,
and the Ontario Publishing Centre.

Canadian Cataloguing in Publication Data

Winter, Michael, 1965-
    Creaking in their skins

ISBN 1-55082-112-1

    I. Title.

PS8595.I624C74 1994   C813'.54   C94-900597-5
PR9199.3.W46C74 1994

Design Consultant: Keith Abraham. Cover art is a detail from a pavement
c. 500 A.D. housed in The Great Palace (Mosaic Museum), Istanbul,
Turkey.

Printed and bound in Canada by Webcom Limited, Toronto, Ontario.

Published by Quarry Press, Inc.,
P.O. Box 1061, Kingston, Ontario K7L 4Y5.

For *Gaile*

∎ ∎ ∎
Contents

■ ■ ■

■ ■ ■

Who hath put wisdom in the inward parts?
or who hath given understanding to the heart?

Job 38:36

Enlarged To Show Texture

■ ■ ■

Pam: I need to know if you have moments of hope for us.

Yutian thinks the further inside he gets the closer he'll be to the visceral. He wants to discover her essence, the truth of her feeling. If he feathers the bump just over her vagina she will respond, but he is never sure if such response is genuine. He has no gauge for authenticity. When Ningsha plays with his cock, he feels a warmth inside. He lies inert, relaxed, allowing the rhythm of her pulls or sucks to melt through him. It is the closest he has come to true meditation. That tenderness vibrating from the core of him.

When his penis is soft it is small and pliable. He can push it into itself, into the bag of scrotum until the finger is half submerged in the dough. When it stiffens, the veins and blood hook it like a banana. The hood slides off and the army cap strains and shines in the purple heat, enlarged to show potential. Is her tunnel so hooked? When he enters from behind, her thighs apart, his hands pressing her buttocks, is his curve sliding inwards, towards her backbone, while her tunnel curves towards her breasts? He has always had trouble with location.

He knows it is more comfortable for Ningsha if he crouches over her back, leaning on the pebbles of her spine, so that his shaft relieves pressure on her inner wall. Are dogs more comfortable with the arc of their mating?

Yutian's view of her from behind is much like his view of her vagina, looking between her legs, knees bent. Her whole body turns into an image he knows she cannot see. She is, for the instant, as weak as a masturbator. Her body a hand, the muscle of her clitoris the flesh of a palm. But it is not his hand — the double touch of flesh that knows flesh, of nerves in the hand and penis recognizing one another. The familiarity of cell tissue is not here. It is a foreign hand, a pulsing larger-than-life glove that folds over his organ, clenching it tight. She does not like this position for that very reason. She senses what she is missing, and what he gains selfishly through her loss. I won't masturbate you, she thinks, and squeezes him out as she recognizes how his scrotum contracts, the tense quiver in his thighs before orgasm.

Someone in the house must masturbate. Richard had thought this because he recognized the state of the bathtub drain from when he used to pull himself in the shower. Sperm clings to hair, choking the drain tines. This week it is his turn to clean the bathroom. A perfect droplet of blood beside the toilet, splashing out to form a Mandelbrot set. Inside the seat, where his penis would rest, another spot of blood. From the bathtub drain he pulls quantities of hair matted with grey sperm. Is it Bill or Yutian? It must be Yutian, for Bill seems happy enough with Kim. But does happiness matter? Yutian has only just started seeing Ningsha. Richard does not know what role masturbation plays with Chinese. But then another possibility: it could be from washing after sex. Bill with a vasectomy can ejaculate inside of Kim. Bouryana uses a diaphragm. Both Richard and Yutian use condoms. Either Kim or Bouryana could squat in the shower and wash the sperm into the drain. That made sense. Hair meshed with sperm from various heads. His own. Pam's. Bouryana, Yutian, Kim and Bill. The coils twist together as he flushes the toilet. He wipes the dried blood and wonders whose period it is. All three women, because of pheromones, have the same cycle.

The cat likes nuzzling into Richard's armpits. At first he thought she was remembering her mother and looking for the nipple. But one day he found her rolling in a frenzy in one of his t-shirts. Rubbing her head into the sweat of an armpit. It is the celery scent of his sweat that attracts her.

Their love is tender and familiar. It is a recognition of old signposts, of the joy of visiting home — a Christmas reunion. They are not calm lovers, not fluid. Their clumsy attempts, that tangle of legs and twist of waists, the heaviness of their parts on each other is not denied. Pam wipes the bead of jism from the mouth of his cock before sucking. Richard strokes away the white curd that builds up on her clitoris. Sometimes they ask each other to wash, the smell too raw. She has learned to hold the base of his cock, to lengthen her throat with the tunnel of her palm, so he feels the pressure to the rim, to the roots of his pubic hair. At the height of their agony they stop and search for her green pouch, which holds the condoms and the spermicidal foam. He shakes the can while she tears open a package. He fills the plastic plunger with the foam and they exchange preparations. "I hate this." She coaxes the hard tube into her vagina. Sometimes, in the poor light of evening, Richard attempts to peel the condom on inside out. He fears to use it then, to turn it over and roll it down. He imagines a smear of semen spreading over the latex, penetrating her egg.

Richard's lips have been bothering him. They have sores inside, against the gums and teeth. Drinking coffee aggravates them. He thinks they come from cunnilingus. Pam tends to rock as he licks with the flat of his tongue and his lips often bang against his teeth. "It could be that," he told her, "or just sleeping on my mouth." His gums are receding, leaving edges on his canines which dig into his lips. He finds he cannot smile properly.

Pam has decided to compromise on the question of growing old together. Whenever she mentions the future it's on the long side of short term. As she says 'us' and Christmas and 'us' and May, it brings that possibility closer, and she knows it makes it harder for Richard to deny it. She will ride his drifting, steer him into old age. They will be there before he knows it.

When Richard buys condoms he checks the expiry date and the safety seal. He won't pick a box that has been exposed to fluorescent lighting. A red sign beside the condom shelf: Open 'til midnight 7 days a week. He prefers giving exact change or money enough so that he can receive whole change in return. A package of twelve goes for $5.88, including tax. He hands the cashier six thirteen. As he passes her the loon, dime and three pennies from his pocket, a pubic hair accompanies them. She flicks it away deftly and gives him back a quarter, pressing the rim of the coin into his palm so that none of her fingers touch his.

When they were in Bulgaria they bought foreign condoms. They searched long for German, but ended up with what looked like a Bulgarian attempt to mimic a German product. "They're too cheap," Richard said, imagining semen leaking through the porous latex wall like so many political refugees. They turned out to be as tough as balloons, the odor of latex overpowering. He withdrew quickly after ejaculation, the caught sperm sagging in two inches of stretched condom. "They're just like my tights," Pam said. Turkish tights that stretched at the knees after one bend. They were in Bouryana's parents' house in Varna on the Black Sea coast. They'd been travelling for three months through Greece and Turkey. Mr and Mrs Brakalova were astonished to see them. Friends of Bouryana who live with her in Canada. There were photographs of Bouryana in downtown St. John's stuck in the corners of glass doors on the parlor bureau. Bouryana standing beside six foot snowdrifts on Pratt Avenue. Bouryana in the backyard with the dogberry bush. The points of pickets rounded by the boys in the field retrieving foul balls. The grass is hay and a few stray perennials lazily line the neighbor's fence. A rusting frame of a chair sits in the middle of the hay, like a car wreck you find in the field alone. There's a mattress leaning against the oil tank. Richard had meant to spraypaint MAKE LOVE NOT WAR on it and hang it from the barrel of the howitzer protecting City Hall. In the background is their bedroom window and, above it, Yutian's. Bouryana with Richard and the rest of the Pratt crew: Yutian, Kim, Bill, the cat.

Mrs Brakalova dug out Bouryana's slippers for Pam. They slept in Bouryana's childhood bed. It was at this moment that Pam asked Richard if he would marry her.

Kim and Bill are newly-weds. They went to Cuba for their honeymoon. Bill said no-one's heard of Capablanca. "Your most famous chess player. World champion." Couldn't even find the chess club in Havana. Kim brought back a tin of cookies for Jose Luis, a colleague at work. Jose said he'd never seen such a cookie tin. He and his wife Galina cannot return to Cuba, so they take interest in the photos Kim and Bill have of the island. 50's cars and tourist beaches. Museums that were once private estates. There is a picture of Bill singing 'My Way' with a Cuban dance band. They had dealt in American dollars. Bill compares Cuba to Miami and never to Haiti.

Kim is a physiotherapist. She works in a psychiatric ward. She's seen a manic depressive go around the floor giving blow-jobs. There was an AIDS patient she had to treat. "I've worked with old people, people with Tourettes, MS and MR patients and in seven years I've never had any body fluids come in contact with me. Well maybe a bit of spit. But when I knew I had an AIDS patient, all I could think of was he's going to slice his wrists and spray blood all over me."

Bill a grandfather. He's forty-two but looks twenty-eight. Except his ears, which he covers with hair. A three year old grandson. Sometimes his daughter calls long distance from Hamilton. Bill trained collies then, had a mortgage and worked shifts in a fabric plant. He turned oil into cloth. He met his first wife in a pool room and they were married six weeks later. But his passion is opera, which he sings. After eight years and two kids he had to go. He works as an optician and has a chance to go partners on the chain store they operate. A framed optical dispensing diploma in the living room.

Kim got a ride home with Jose Luis. "One of my biggest fears just happened. I dread the thought of getting a lift home because I know I won't be able to explain where Pratt is. I had Jose going in circles, zigzagging all over town. I lose all direction when I'm in a car. It goes too fast for my sense of place."

On her lunch break Kim had bought a photo album for the amateur pictures of her wedding. In the cover is an oval inset with a picture of a generic couple standing under an autumn tree. Slashed through them like a pennant is a diagonal yellow strip. Along it reads 'Sample Only — Place Your Photo Here'.

Kim is disappointed with the professional photos. "The ones of Bill are great. But me, I don't know. I knew this would happen, because when I saw she was going to take a picture I'd put on the look that I wanted, and I'd hold my look waiting for her to take the picture. And just after I'd lost my look is when she'd take the fucking thing."

Bill and Kim play hockey twice a week. They rent the ice at Hoyle's Arena every Tuesday and Friday. Bill lacks the stamina to stay on the ice more than a minute.

"I can't keep the pace, or exert too much. As soon as I get the puck I rush with it and then have to pass off. And the other team knows it. Two minutes and I'll faint."

It's because of his legs. Blood pools in them, starving the rest of his body. Three years ago he had a clot in the largest artery in his waist. His legs slowly thickened. His doctor told him to eat aspirin. On the third day his legs are twice their normal size. "Ninety centimeters in diameter." He was admitted and they administered a blood thinner. Antibodies began to puncture a hole through the clot and dissolve it. They sent him home. "I thought I was going to die. Really. And then Roy Orbison died."

It took three weeks for his legs to return to normal. During that time his secondary veins and arteries had taken over, had enlarged. "And they remember. They don't want to give up." They're still larger than normal and stand out on his stomach and chest like speedbumps. "Now the main veins in my legs have no flaps to push the blood back to the heart. They expanded so much the flaps split apart."

Kim said when they got engaged, the talk at work always revolved around setting a date. "I must say I felt pressured from them to get a day out of Bill. Now that we're married it's assumed the little one's on its way."

Bill with a fourteen-year-old vasectomy. Recently he'd been looking into getting a reversal. "It'd be nice to have our own." They're not hopeful. Richard is waiting for rubber implants to come on the market. "I'll bank some sperm just in case."

Bouryana: It beats taking hormones.

Kim asks Bouryana which photo she likes of Kim and her bridesmaid. Bouryana chooses one deep in the back: an outdoor shot with hair blown by the wind. Kim points this out. "I can't send Tina one with my hair like that. I mean it's not what you think of when you think of a wedding picture."

Bouryana is excited. Her Landed Immigrant Status came in the mail. She can now apply for her MCP card. She can look for work. She did a Masters in marine biology in Varna. "I could do research at the university. Study baby scallops." She's already got her resume in for three different positions. She's done a lot of lab work with electron microscopes. "Things are never larger than they are. They just appear closer to us."

At the moment, she sees Tom. Tom a fisheries observer. He can be out on a foreign trawler for up to six weeks. He's there to check their quota. He was over for supper once. "It's a dull job. You get a lot of reading done." He said it's different out there. "You're the foreigner on board. International waters. No Canadian law. Everything you leave behind is frozen until you get back. You're stuck in a moment while everyone here is moving ahead without you. The worst is when it's too rough to make it back to Burin. You just got to stay out there, waiting. Your worst enemy is land."

Bouryana doesn't know it yet, but tonight in bed crab lice will hatch out of the eggs Tom has planted in her pubic hair. She will spend tomorrow scratching herself before noticing the flakes of flesh moving in slow motion, crawling blindly but with purpose through the forest of smooth black trunks of pubic hair. A second before she will not see them and then out of the normalness of her crotch they will appear, dozens of flat crabs creeping like tanks through their territory. A doctor will prescribe a topical cream which she'll apply twice, ten days apart. She will wash her bed linen, nightgowns and panties. She will vacuum her mattress.

That morning, a courier had dropped off the wedding video. Kim plans to show it that night. "I'll make fish soup." With one of the wedding presents — a Sears gift certificate — Kim bought a top-of-the-line food processor. Only Bouryana showed a liking for it. The processor towers over the toaster and leaves little counter space. Kim can use it on the vegetables. Bill has bought vodka, gin, and tonic water. He also hauls out a 40-ouncer of rum from their Cuba trip. "To celebrate Bouryana. A Landed Immigrant like me." Bill was born in the States.

The Pratt crew in attendance. Tom still aboard a Soviet trawler. "He's probably in Iceland," Bouryana says sadly. While eating the soup, Bill pulled a pen light from his shirt pocket. "Shine it in your eye. The light reflects on your retina back to the cornea. You can see the path of blood vessels in behind your eye." Richard tried it. The view was maroon with wrinkles of blue. A dry riverbed, the mud cracked into deep chunks.

They start in on the rum. Bouryana cheers up, flashing her immigration papers and ID. "Some Bulgarians they are a little disappointed in Canada. Their expectations are very high. But I didn't hope too much. I remember the officials at Gander airport, they thought I'd be kissing the ground. 'You must feel like you're in Paradise,' one said. I said 'No, just Canada. In winter.'"

Kim reaches for Bill's hand. "We've got some bad news. Medical news." She stares at Bill's eyes. "We won't be having children."

"Well there's all sorts of having children."

"Yes well, we won't be having any that'll be ours."

"The doctor said up to eight years and you have a chance.

But after that the vas deferens deteriorate drastically, so I'd just be shooting immature sperm."

"And the other thing is Bill's condition. They don't want to risk another clot."

They watch the video in the dark on Yutian's VCR. If he cannot extend his Fellowship he will have to sell the VCR along with his car. Four of them share the couch. Fleas run through the cat's fur and, at times, feed off Pam and Kim. The highlight of the video is when Bill sings "Some Enchanted Evening" at the altar while Kim and her father listen at the top of the aisle. Bill sings with an accent, rolling the r's. *Acrrross a crrrowded rrroom.* When Pam asks him why he does this he says "I learned the song in Italian."

The half-empty bottles and glasses encircle the chessboard. An unfinished game. Bill has Richard in zugzwang. Yutian mentions that four of the top ten female players are Chinese. "I think in China women are brought up to be more analytical." Near the end of the video Bouryana leaves the room. When Pam comes back from the bathroom she whispers to Richard that Bouryana is crying in the porch with the phone. "I think it's about Tom." As the video closes with scenes from the reception, Bill opens the flue and starts a fire. He throws on bits of broken chair along with coal Bouryana has collected from the bottom of Trinity Bay. From time to time he pours a margarine tubful onto the embers. The coal has fragments of coral attached. They all sit silent, watching the pulse of red and orange amid the black core.

Richard and Pam sleep in the room below Yutian. They used to have Yutian's room, before they left for eastern Europe. Yutian's footsteps make the light shade jingle on its mounting. Yesterday Richard had told him about the noise. Yutian said he would like China. "Very considerate. You could teach English there. Live a very simple life. In a village in the south, near Nepal. It would have to be a high school. No electricity. You'd heat and cook with wood."

After the coal is consumed Richard goes to bed. Pam comes in much later and wakes him with her cold feet. Richard: Did I miss much?

"Kim and Bouryana threw up in the bathroom. I found them on the floor, leaning against the bathtub. They were counting how many boyfriends they'd had who'd thrown up in bed. That's what Kim had just done and I could hear Bill whistling, turning the mattress over. Bouryana looked really sad. She mentioned the brown eggs in the fridge. She said her great aunt wouldn't touch a brown egg. Her husband was a Nazi. He had to go into hiding after the war. She never saw him again and ever since she's avoided anything brown. We all laughed at that. She said she's got no energy. Sleeps twelve hours a day."

Pam spoons into him. He can feel the pad taped to her underwear. She says, "You know I feel jealous. I like Bouryana, but I can't get too close to her. Because I know you're fond of her. That's why, when you told me she liked the idea of Kim getting a food processor, at first I thought how odd, but then I was glad because I knew you couldn't be that fond of someone who likes food processors."

Richard has had two affairs. One was five years ago, the other three. He quickly told Pam about the second one. But it was only recently and indirectly that Pam found out about the first. It was with a mutual friend. Pam has since lost her trust. She cannot see Richard with another woman without wondering if they have slept together. This has affected Richard, who feels frustrated that his attempts at fidelity mean nothing because of two nights of lost faith.

"I don't get depressed over it . . . and I don't have any pride left. I'm just grieving . . . over this relationship. I'm grieving over the loss." He can feel the quiver in her voice. "I made a choice, I chose you and you're telling me, the man I love, that you don't want me. . . . You won't marry me." She turns away from him to face the wall. "I'm sad because I want to see you grow old."

At times Richard has wanted Bouryana, as he has longed for many naked bodies. It annoys him for he knows he has a partner of character. But he wants to wander, to lie in alien beds, to wake up in different parts of the world that have no connection except through him. He wants a checkered past, several separate lives in the one fold of living given to him. If I stay with her, he thinks, it will mean one life. His wish is that they had met in their thirties.

He has willed Bouryana past his door, occasionally ached for her to knock. They've eyed each other appreciatively. The sexual tension resulting from this has been noticed by Pam. She has warned Richard that the natural obstacles that separate Bouryana from him could vanish. "You're not safe together in this house."

They were almost asleep when they woke to the sound of friction. The mattress above them rubbing against the wall. Ningsha's small moans are perfect and near. Both Richard and Pam feel tight. "It's hard not to listen, isn't it?" Not to imagine their tense, sinewy bodies; their mustard-brown skins. Ningsha's alert, small breasts and Yutian's serious, leathery cock. "Just after you left, I saw Yutian groping Ningsha. He was really rude. She left the room over it."

After a long time, longer than Richard could sustain with Pam, Yutian ejaculated into the quiet of their moment. A few Mandarin words, some laughing, and then footsteps to the bathroom; the toilet flushed and the taps whined.

"If we'd heard them having tea in the kitchen we could join them. But sex, you can't let them know you've noticed." Pam hugs Richard and they relax into easy sleep.

The cat butts the door open and stares at them. It watches as they breathe in the excrement of billions of dust mites. Chewing skin from pillows. Breeding, infesting, dying. The weight of arms over floating lungs and the stale exhalations of breath keep Richard and Pam apart. The cat trots over to Richard's laundry pile. Flea eggs sense the vibration of her feet. They hatch from instinct and with their only muscle leap into the air.

They get up late. Yutian and Ningsha are in the kitchen drinking tea. Richard drives a few slices of bread into the toaster. Lifts the cereal box from the top of the fridge.

Yutian: Are you cooking tonight?

"No. Monday."

"We will cook then. We have something important to announce. We are going to marry."

"Wow. Congratulations. So quick."

"Well, we are sure."

They leave them to their cereal and toast. As they eat, Richard notices the picture on the cereal box. In small print beside the bowl it says Enlarged To Show Texture. The bowl is magnified, the bran flakes three times their normal size. A larger-than-life spoon plunges into the bowl, splashing globs of glue-like milk onto the deep blue background. Three huge raspberries are stuck onto the cereal. Their shadows betray the artwork collage which has gone into this breakfast. It is effective from a distance, on a shelf while one is walking down the aisle. But up close it looks contrived and artificial.

Two Families

■ ■ ■

I hold her in the kitchen. She's eating a carrot and the crunch of the carrot runs through the skull, enters my chin resting on her red hair. It's hard to tell if I hear the crunch or feel it. The bones move in her skull. The muscle across her temples.

At the table the sun runs through her teeth. You can see the stumps of the teeth beneath the enamel, as if it's her baby teeth, teeth I've seen tumble out of her mouth. She's laughing as I tell her about feeling her skull. And now I tell her about the teeth.

I've known Bev from birth. I tell her things she can't remember. I saw her take the first steps. We called Hubert in. He fell to his knees. Come on Bevy, he said. And Bev all wide eyes fell towards him, running into her fall as Hubert caught her. And Ben and me watching his sister and his father holding each other on the carpet in the house I used to live in.

When we showed the house the closets hadn't been partitioned. Ben and I weaved from room to room through the passages. My father had built a new house on land to the right and we moved into that. So when I played at Ben's I was in my old house. My new bedroom was straight across from my old. Ben and I could talk through the windows. At

night, I viewed my old window — the clear yellow-orange
picture of the built-in desk, Ben sitting there, the wallpaper
— saw it all from a new angle. My sister taught us sign language to save our lungs.

Ben's mother had the job. She worked shifts at the
Bowater mill office. She took salt tablets. Mr Callahan said
Call me Hubert, and so distinguished himself from the start.

Hubert's work changed with the weather. On good days
in summer he hunted, fished, or cut wood. On bad he shifted
boxes in a warehouse. In the fall he loaded herring aboard
Russian trawlers. You could see the good meat on his arms.

He showed Ben and me how to steam birch in a long
pipe, how to bend it into snowshoes, how to fill the shoes
with orange twine. He let us take turns melting the frayed
end of twine with a match. He wetted his fingers to mold the
flame into a black nub.

At seven Ben told me he was going to have a wife. His
mother was big. In time he'd grow up and marry his new sister.

You mean I have to marry my sister?

Who was seven years older. And Ben said he supposed
that's how it worked.

I watched the baby grow. She was quiet. Ben said you could
stamp on her foot and she wouldn't yell. And her head. She
banged doors open.

Ben took me down to Mount Moriah where his cousins
lived. In summer we played baseball in the field behind his
Nan's. Winter they cleared a patch of the bay for hockey. I
wasn't much good but Ben said If Marshall doesn't play then
I don't. I could never get used to the boom of the ice.

We'd warm up at his Nan's. Her house right on the
water. My own grandparents lived too far away to see regu-
larly. My mother was angry when I signed a Christmas card

to her parents, With all my love, Marshall Abbott.

Ben's Nan wore a baseball cap with a pompom. She split her own wood. Five cords of wood cut by her five sons. Even jigged a few fish when the water was right. Pop's old dory in the yard beside Hubert's inboard. There were pictures all over, of Pop and Hubert and lots of Ben and Bev and their cousins. Nothing on the walls but photos of family.

I had thirteen children, she told me. Nine alive. Seven still living. Leo and Peter were lost when the gasoline exploded. All they found was the skiff and a body. Hubert had to go down to identify it, she said. All he could recognize was the lifejacket melted into the back. That's Leo, Hubert said. They never found Peter.

Hubert took us out in the boat. Had us over Paddy's Ledge. Handed me a jigger. Down to the bottom then up one length. I had a fish on for an hour and didn't know it. Hubert cleaned it over the side, the gulls gliding in for the guts. He fried the fillets on a hot plate by the motor. The boat swaying gently as we ate squares of hot white cod. Then Hubert peed over the gunnel, a thick yellow arch.

As Bev got older my sister babysat. She said Bev was reasonable in her own way, but stubborn. At midnight Bev wanted a cheese and olive sandwich and Ann would try to tell her she should be asleep, but the sandwich had to be made. And fourteen olives too. She preferred to sleep on the couch while Ann watched TV.

I tell this to Bev now and she shakes her head: I don't even like olives.

My father liked Hubert. They went partners on a moose. My father a big man, from building. And Hubert a keener. He had an edge my father liked, a blunt edge he jammed against things. He wanted to go a week early, during the crossbow hunt.

But you don't know how to shoot an arrow, Hubert.

It's easy, Tim. You down a moose with a slug. You shove an arrow in its neck.

On top of a hill on the transmission line. Hubert is pointing to the American Man. He wants to climb to the Station. My father carries binoculars. He tells Hubert to have a look.

Geez, you can see everything.

Hubert checks the valley, amazed. He hands them back.

You saved me an afternoon's walk, Tim.

On the barren in the hut by the railway tracks. Ben and me and our fathers. The hut is shingled with plastic realty signs from one of Hubert's brothers. Finest kind of roof. For half a mile you can see those blue, yellow and orange For Sale signs beaming over the barrens. It's your fourth day and the train is due. The food has gone and it's time to return. But there's still partridge. Without a word Hubert goes for the garbage. He picks out the potato peelings and you put on a pan of water. You boil the peelings and stay another day.

Ben and me alone with my father. We were camping in Little Grand Lake and we had our food rationed. We had it in grocery bags stuffed into the ends of our kayaks. We brought cartons of eggs. One morning Ben and I were cooking breakfast and the frying pan slid off the wood and the eggs and bacon slipped into the sand. It was funny to see. The eggs so perfect, sitting on the sand. My father flew at us. He shoveled the eggs and bacon back into the pan and said Eat it. He made us eat it. The sand in our teeth. And we're sitting there trying to cry as quietly as we can eating sandy bacon and eggs. Hubert wouldn't have done that. And we've got to spend four more days with this man.

MICHAEL WINTER

A story my mother does not know. Of my father and
Hubert in the boat on Grand Lake. Two moose quartered.
The waves rise. The boat is gunnel to. The waves swamp.
The boat is no longer of the air. You note the exact moment
the transition occurs. From floating to sinking. The boat lifts
on a wave then flips. You try for the surface but your arm is
snagged in the rope. You see the sky but the anchor weighs
you down. Your boots fill up. Your clothing bloats. It's October.
The surface is just there. The boat. Then you're caught on
something. It hooks you around the waist. It tears you from
the rope. It lifts you from the water and it's Hubert. It's Hubert
dragging you to the beach. He lays you in the surf. A quarter of
moose is trapped in a bubble beneath the boat. He hauls that
up too. This is a story your father tells in a whisper, alone.
When you're fishing and he tells you how his wrist still hurts.

This is Bev's story:
    Hubert is the seventh son of a seventh son.
    But if you talk to Nan he's not the one. The seventh son
was a girl. She was born dead and they called her Josephine
and had a little wake. And after, when they had to sign the
papers, they found the mistake.
    The girl is a boy so you should change the name.
    And so Nan called him Joseph Josephine and that's how
Hubert became the seventh son, but really the eighth. People
couldn't remember if Joseph Josephine was a girl or a boy, or
they forgot him all together and so when Hubert came along,
the seventh son they called him. But Nan said No, Joseph
Josephine is the seventh. There was an open tolerance for
that but people kept waiting on Hubert. They silently kept a
watch on him. People brought warts. A blind woman wanted
Hubert to touch her cataracts. A family took a lame girl to the
house. And Hubert couldn't work a thing. Fourteen and a

26

failure. And Nan said It's Joseph Josephine they want. Don't ever try it again, Hubert. You can't be a failure if you do what you're cut out for.

Bev has a scar from her nose to her lip. Many take it for a harelip, but it's a scar from a fall. Her front teeth cracked at the gums and she has a picture of her sideways smile with the gap and it's a picture I want a copy of. The teeth are capped but the color isn't right. A fault line runs through them. There is a scar on her elbow from the same fall and so the elbow and the lip are connected. I kiss the lip and the elbow. I neglect the other elbow. The kiss is a solace. For something that happened before me.

Although I was there. I remember the fall. There are dents in the wooden stairs from her teeth, stairs my father built.

Ben and I were in the basement loading shot, crimping shells to use at the Rod and Gun Club. And Bev, kneeling on the steps, watched through the gaps. Watched us make shells.

Ben and I worked the trap shoot. Hubert had shown us how to load the clay pigeons. The mechanical arm slowly rotating, reversing. Unpredictable. The massive spring coiled, the shout, *PULL!*, and the arm cracking out of the trap. The fluorescent disk gliding over the clearing, a shotgun blast behind us and the pigeon splintering, or escaping to coast out to the curtain of trees.

We collected the missing, stacked them. We gathered the spent shells. And these we reloaded in Hubert's basement. We replaced the copper pin, packed in gunpowder, crammed in the plastic wadding, the shot, and finally crimped the end. We could tell by the weight what size pellet we'd used. What kind of bird we could down.

We heard the fall. Bev's mouth hitting the edge of each step, her teeth splintering. A trail of blood. Falling to the painted concrete floor. No-one there to catch her.

That winter Nan was chopping splits. We could see her from the ice. She wore Pop's old parka. She was splitting birch. Putting the wedge in and banging it with the butt of the axe-blade. She fills a grocery cart, then wheels it in.

She got in the kitchen when her back started to sweat, she said. She felt all musty inside and she tried to undo the parka, but she couldn't get it down. The zipper got stuck. And the heat was getting to her. She opened the stove door to throw in a junk and all she could think of was, I'm going to collapse here and now and the stove is going to jump out and I'll be all burnt up in Pop's parka. Like Leo and Peter. And she tugged at the zipper but her fingers were numb. Her back was hot but her fingers were cold from the axe. So she tried to sit down on the table edge. She was getting hotter and she felt like she was going to suffocate. Her breath came faster. And then a voice came, a little whisper like from a two-year old that said, Mommy pull the coat over your head like Daddy does his sweater. And Nan said I wouldn't have thought of that in a hundred years. I was so caught up in the zipper. So first I wriggled my arms out and then I shucked it over my head. Sweat peeling off me. And I said Thank-you Joseph Josephine.

Seven years is not a big gap. I know couples who are twenty years apart. And to think a man of twenty watching a new baby and saying, Someday I'll marry her, is odd. But if they meet when they're older not much is said about age.

I tease Bev about the crush she had on me. She would brush against me, move in for a kiss. Fiddle with my hair. Draw hearts with our names along the shaft of an arrow. It was embarrassing for Ben. I didn't know how to handle it.

We were finishing high school. Once, when we were drinking in the woods, I asked Ben how far he'd gone and he said with Louise he had two fingers up. And after I didn't see so much of Ben. We were driven apart by a word, an idea. We wanted the outfield and a cousin said, Let the fags have it. That word drove in between us. You had to watch what you looked like.

We weren't in the same classes. I didn't go to hockey. He stopped looking out his window. I watched him nail a pole up the side of the house and secure an antenna. I saw his silhouette on the curtain with the CB radio Hubert gave him for Christmas. Talking to everyone in the world except me.

In the fall I left for university. Ben opted for a trade. It was those missing years I couldn't fill in. While I was gone Bev hit her teens. Ben said she'd started going to church. The Salvation Army had her attention. She wore the uniform and read the Bible. Ben had always figured Bev would be something strange, but this he hadn't reckoned on. He couldn't kid her. She was dead serious. And then in high school she finished with it. Didn't have a word for God. She started wandering. You could spot her from a distance. A small town doesn't hold too many strange ones. She would walk between the maples in Bowater Park. She'd climb the hill above West Street, the glue sniffers behind her. The boys called her Beaver. Easy tail.

At sixteen she moved in with Nan, who needed someone. That's the story. Bev slept upstairs in Pop's old bed while Nan kept to the living room. Her sons built a bathroom off the kitchen so Nan never had to take a stair again. Bev would help her up when she wanted to look out over the bay, see the newsprint ships coasting in. The island she grew up on standing at the horizon.

I was home that summer, a B.A. but no job. I helped my father build a new house up Bayview Heights. Ben had gotten his interprovincial papers, two cars in the shed. He never heard of a muffler, my mother said. The racket. He took me out in his Datsun. He was looking for a good accident to get insurance money. He had gotten fatter, the bones in his face had widened. We both felt sorry for not keeping close.

He said his cousin was getting married and Bev had no-one to go with and she always had a good thing to say about me. We could all go in his car so I wouldn't have to be alone. He was still with Louise, in fact they were engaged now after splitting up twice. He said as soon as he got on to one of the garages they'd find a spot and settle. He said he liked the houses my old man was building. Great view.

She had changed since her crush. She had been flat chested, wild. Her lank red hair fell flat across her shoulders. She'd worn Ben's old jeans. Now her hair was short, wedged. She still wore jeans, but with tank-tops that showed. She used mascara but not lipstick. She hadn't gone to her grad.

At the wedding she wore a dress she found at Nan's. Imagine. She wore this. She had thirteen kids and wore this.

It was a simple dress. Blue cotton. Nan had sewn it on the foot-pedaled Singer. Dyed it in the tub. The dress fit Bev perfectly.

Bev and I sat with Nan at the banquet. You could place a spirit level upon their heads and watch the bubble sit dead center.

We wore the aluminum rings that held the napkins.

Bev wasn't sure what to do with her life. She was coasting. When Hubert lost his license she often drove to town to take her mother to work. Late at night they'd drive back along the Shore, the bay flat, the lights from places you thought no-one lived. Mrs Callahan preferred the radio off and stared out the door. And Bev could see the tired look in her mother. Her frame settling into the seat. After parking she'd watch her mother through the opaque glass in the porch, tugging off her shoes. Hanging her coat. Then she'd watch the smoke climbing out of the chimney and think of that house rooted as firmly as the trees it burned.

I'd spy from my window. If it was okay Bev would give a sign. We'd take the road along the water. I'd remind her about the high beam.

At Nan's we took the stairs to Pop's room. We'd kiss and touch. She'd say No, let me. Let me do it, and I'd let her decide things. If I tried to undo her shirt or her bra she'd whisper No, don't. And she would undo it.

We put the blankets on the floor because the bed creaked. I had to lie on my back. Bev leaned over me, her hands on my shoulders as if holding me there. Then she'd feel for my penis. From blue window light she'd unroll a condom as I kissed her nipples, one breast slightly larger. When she was ready she'd guide herself on.

As she rocked she stared at me. She never closed her eyes. She stared as she shivered and exhaled hard. She wouldn't take me in her mouth or let me reach down with my tongue. She had to see my eyes. Know who I was. We could use fingers as long as the eyes held.

She said there were a lot of guys, but in the car. She couldn't bring them here. They'd go to Bowater Park and use the gazebo. She'd had an infection last summer and that had frightened her. But it turned out benign. She had to get her uterine walls frozen and the cells flushed out.

We told stories. She knew much more about my mother than I did. About when she went to visit Mrs Callahan she'd take two spoons of sugar but hardly stir her tea. When Mrs

Callahan remarked at the silt my mother would say, I'm never sure how sweet I'll like it. This way I can stir it until it suits me and I don't have to ask for more.

I asked about the Sally Ann. About what had happened there, but Bev shook her head. I kept asking until she raised an eyebrow with an impatient stare.

Okay, she said. You want to know? Okay.

She said I tried everything. Every way to get him to stop. And the Army was good. I got a reason out of it. He didn't stop but at least I had a reason. I could get my mind off it. And then it was Christmas Eve. I had my uniform on, all ironed. I held my Bible that Captain Tobin had signed over to me and I was about to go when Dad came in. I said You can't rape me now, Dad. I'm going to Assembly. He shut the door and said You think that'll stop me? And I said Dad I've got my uniform on, and he shoved me on the bed, pinned my arms. He burst the buttons off my jacket. He grabbed the Bible, opened it, tore out a few pages and pulled down his pants. He wrapped the paper round his bird. He said I'm God, Bevy. Don't ever forget it. And then he shoved in his bird with the pages wrapped around it.

And so I hold her. I let my chin rest on the top of her head. I feel her breasts under her blouse spread across my stomach and her fingers grip underneath my shoulder blades. I want to see her teeth in the sun. To alter the fault line buried beneath.

Becoming Frank

■ ■ ■

1

My brother Frank was a runner, a long distance runner. He ran over every road in town, the city map covered, then he ran into the hills. The woods roads and transmission lines. He couldn't get enough road into his lungs. When you run you can ignore rules, you can run with the traffic, cross on the Don't Walk, run oneway streets the wrong way, break the speed limit (a runner's goal). He reached the Top 30 in Canada and that was it. All he could do. Started driving. Motorbikes, Datsuns, Beetles, and Rabbits. He drove like he ran, an erratic habit, and he slipped further into his own rules.

He took flying lessons, wanted to be a busher. They grounded him for going under power lines. I'm sure his way seemed normal enough to him, but you get acting strange so often it makes you see screwy, your sights are crooked. You think you're shooting straight but you're four feet off the mark. And if someone brings you back to the bull's-eye, it feels uncomfortable. You liked shooting at the periphery.

2

I understand. You want a physical description. Contents of the room as last seen. I found him sleeping. His boots were drying on the open oven door. Bottom element was cranked up, orange as a forge. Curtains closed, thin ones you could see the day through. Roaster on the stove with two chickens picked over in it. Nothing on the kitchen table except a pack of smokes and a salt shaker. And a tiny wrench. A stripped-down V-8 between the table legs. '57 Bel Air, I think. Spare tire on the kitchen counter. Two fifty dollar bills thumb-tacked to the wall. Box of condoms on the toilet. Hotdogs and a bottle of Baby Duck in the fridge. Out back the TV was still there. Up against the shed by the beat-up bonnet. We put it out last week. Big floor model. He said it only got one channel. It was raining and it felt wrong, the water on the wood. All those wires inside.

③

Remember Joe the black and white Dad brought to dump and I snuck the gun? We followed him on the 650 Honda and we stopped on a red and Chris Murray saw the 12 gauge on my back and asked and I said We're going to rob a bank. The gulls, the fat gulls in the garbage thousands of them picking them off with number 4 shell and that huge granddaddy one I got with a slug. He disappeared they couldn't learn, Joe. Wings they wouldn't use just check out what's in the pick-up and they're hopping on the tailgate and me with a bead on 'em.

And there's Dad with the boulder. The TV all alone without the living room around it. Car wrecks, plastic, picking through for rims and axles. Pieces no-one knows how to fit together anymore and Dad with the boulder at his waist, swinging it for momentum till I thought He aims to squat a gull, but he heaved it over and through the air to the TV, the boulder passing through the screen, not bouncing off. No power in the TV when the plug's on the ground looking for the living room. Boulder lies half in half out the green screen hanging in triangles and the seagulls on top to see if there's food. But Chris, Where you going? To the bank, I said. What a look!

4

Room smelled pretty bad. Hot and stale from the oven. No, he didn't say much. I remember him rubbing his eyes saying Joe, Joe what a dream, what a dream. And he had this dream where he was on the top floor of this big house, in the dark, but he was familiar with the house. It was his house, the house of his dreams all two stories and an acre of land with a pond attached and a woman in one room and a slew of kids in bunk beds and him proud of the feat with a two-ramp garage and employees. And he knew he was in his bedroom and there was a light above him and a string hanging from it and when he clicked the bulb on he'd find a woman's head below him and Montreal's body in the sheets and he'd climb in beside and say This is all right I can get used to this. But snow on the window blocked any light coming in and though he knew exactly where the string was, when he reached up to turn it on, he couldn't find it. He moved his arm back and forth, his forearm high to increase the area of touch, but he couldn't feel it. He just stood there waving his arm, the darkness around him growing, the walls drifting, the bed fading and the woman falling until he wasn't sure where he was anymore. Then he heard me knocking.

5

Frank did up a van, put a bed in, a sink, a propane stove. I guess he'd been planning to run for a couple of months. He bolted his toolboxes behind the bucket seats. There's no way they can steal the tools without taking the whole van, Joe. The ignition key is a Robertson's screwdriver. Canadian brand. They don't make them in the States. He drove to Daytona, three thousand miles in three days. He sent a letter.

⑥

Somewhere near Daytona. Perhaps in Daytona. Yes, by the 500 speedway, the first in the world. They used to race on the beach in the winter, the beach I face where the sun'll come up in a parking lot of one of the hotels. My van is there still black but soon I'll spray it white the sun too hot it'd melt the paint in March just five minutes from Flagler Beach. Work on a hurricane-proof condo that's just a frame and blueprints. Shovel cement and carry blocks all day a hundred feet from the beach. The boys call me Fireball Roberts after a driver killed who's got a grandstand. Wish I had my Pontiac or something to weave the traffic.

Been here four months just before Christmas with my UI in the bank. At the end of my ballpoint trail down the seaboard south of Jacksonville where that hurricane hit — a hurricane's the severest storm on earth, Joe. There's sure no cities on the southeast coast. Oh man I want a block of land in the woods not too far and build a house — you need money though for windows cement lumber doors, Joe. They cost money no matter how much you build. Shingles wiring.

Paid $40 to drive my van inside the speedway. Watched the Rolex 24 hour race the Japs' Nissan won. They change drivers every so often so he doesn't get tired and fuck up at 200 mph. I think that's less of a sport and one guy should do the entire 24. I take pictures of very fast machines, I go to the airport to shoot the big jets taking off under full power. They land in Gander to refuel. The ocean is still the ocean only not as powerful as ours. I'm here with the geese from our cabin — I'm sure I know some of them, I'd love a gun now. I cook chops and chicken on the barbecue and I wash in the hotel. It's good but it's lonely, I haven't patience to wait in the post office line but I need to hear from my brother, we're tight no matter what, Joe.

Let's just say I blew it with a woman, it's a lonely proposition. The cops they know me now and leave me alone, though they count the geese.

7

This story is not about my brother. That's why I chose 'becoming' in the title. My brother is becoming something, becoming the Frank in this story, perhaps. Nothing is ever anything for long and so if my brother does become Frank, he'll soon not be Frank. In fact, this story never becomes Frank until the end. I have to have Frank dead so that he stops becoming. Perhaps that's why I'm relying on testimony. Cold, written facts; letters; notes. Anything that's fixed, pinned to a time. He was so quick, so hard to hold down for a minute. Like I said, he was into fast things.

8

I fell in love with this car last week, it's a 1953 2-door Chevrolet Power Glide. The guy wants 1800 US. If I can ship it home I could get 5 to 8 'G' for it, so it's an excellent investment. Can you find out how I can stay in the TV for three years, I think you're only allowed to be in for 6 months.

Joe, I believe in God because of what Grandma told me once and the two narrow escapes from death I've had — killing the moose in the Rabbit and hitting the 18-wheeler in the O.D. Also, I nearly got it once while flying in the Cessna and trying to spin the plane more times than the manufacturer's allowance, but I got out of that one myself, I think.

I met this UK guy at the track and he liked my way and loaned me 1500 US to buy the car — I have to have him paid back by April 1st because he's buying a house in the Keys. He just opened his wallet and passed me 15 'C' notes. I have to meet him and his woman at the Daytona 500 Sunday, 16 Feb. If you get the chance watch it on TV and I'll be parked inside the infield, standing on the roof of my van at turn #4.

⑨

She sat on the hood of his pick-up. The hood was hot, from the engine and the sun, and as she lay back against the windshield her bare arms left traces of sweat on the glass. Frank jacked up the wheel with her on the hood. The pick-up looked over the Atlantic. They were in Ferryland past the lighthouse. Frank drove over the grass to the edge. There was very little wind, which is rare. He took out a tiny wrench from his tool box. It shone silver like a caplin with its mouth open. Cute, hey? It looked too tiny to be useful. Be even cuter once it grows up.

Frank met her at the Top and Bottom Club. He was head bouncer and she was a dancer from Montreal. They fly in weekly, do the tour in Corner Brook and St. John's. This guy's got a strip club franchise. She found Frank and wanted to get off cocaine.

The perspiration marks must have done something to the paint because you could see the contour of her rear and her heels on the hood. Two sets of symmetrical shapes mirrored like the print of paint in a fold of paper. I guess the heat baked her into the paint. Like enamel in an oven. You could find Frank looking at those few spots like they were all that was left of her, all that she gave him. And from those few fragments he rebuilt her, idealizing what she had been from the memory left to him.

When he totalled the pick-up in a head-on with a Big Wheels transport he was good about it. He salvaged the engine and transmission for the van and cannibalized the rest. He hauled the bent-up hood off its hinges. The F and the R had always been missing from the front. My O.D. pick-up. Now all the letters were gone, a no-name brand. He didn't use the bonnet again, just leaned it up against the side of the shed. The cracks through the finish rusted the marks she had left in the paint, and finally one day he looked and she was gone.

When Frank got his interprovincial papers, he left for Montreal. He found a job and got his tools sent up. Had to put them on the subway from the train station. One and a half tons of tools, Joe. And I'm dragging them around on the metro. I was just lucky none of the casters broke. The job lasted three months and then he was back. Came back alone.

10

You can tell a lot about someone through little things. Like Frank's three drains had no plugs. His kitchen sink, bathroom sink and bathtub drain. I pointed this out and he said No, Joe I guess I don't. He wasn't surprised or saying Yes I've been meaning to get some. Plugs weren't important to him. He didn't have a reason to hold water. He showered, he washed dishes under the faucet, and to shave he ran the taps in the bathroom sink.

It's erosion that moves him. He doesn't create anything. He lives on erosion like water on stone like a river and when you look at it that's what it's about, isn't it? Choked on silt. His force is natural, is all. It's his part to tear things down. You got to live with it. You try taking away what's making him go and there's nothing left. He's supposed to fix things but strength comes from the wreckage. The rust and accidents. The ability to bend, tear and mutilate, that's what he admires. And don't we need it? The decay, the breaking down of things?

11

Didn't get the Chevy it needed too much work. Bought a Pontiac Trans-Am instead — a Turbo 301 cubic inch engine! A racing street car, Joe. I've parked the van to rest it and I tear around town in the car. It's the most powerful I've ever driven. I had to get a Florida

driver's license to get plates and insurance. Then the police would leave
me alone as I'd look like a local and not a tourist. They pick on
Canadians that stay too long, they can lock you up for whatever reason. They arrested me for obtaining a Florida driver's license through
fraud and I spent three days in jail before Dad bonded me out on
$2000. I guess he's not happy about me, but I was trying to be good!

I told them my address was 105 Hamilton, that's my General
Delivery, and they asked me if it was a house or an apartment and I
went for the full thing and said a house and they checked it and
found a post office and then my bunk in the van, so that's that. I
hired a good lawyer for 1600 US and I pray he gets me off this bull-
shit charge. I am thinking about running for home but Dad would
lose his 2000 and I would never be allowed back in the US, but
there's the UK guy too who's looking for his money and I should've
known he was expecting interest. Apparently there's a fixed rate when
you deal at the track.

12

Frank asked about the tire, if he could put something in it. It
was just before he left. I asked him what in particular and he
looked at the fifties and said A package about that size,
maybe six inches thick. So I asked him if it was valuable and
he said Yeah, like of course it is. So I told him maybe he
should put it in the bank or a safety deposit box but he said
No, it's got to go in your spare tire. Like that was it, the only
reasonable place for it. So I said Is it drugs Frank, and he said
No, and I said So it's like the Top and Bottom job, and he
said So you know what it is now, and I said Frank, you were
lucky that time but the cops they know right, they're just
waiting for you to do something extreme. But he's always
talked like that. Always getting on with stuff. See when we
were young he'd tell me things like there were ships in the
sewers. And if you crawl down a manhole you'll see the

decks, the floating teak rails on a river of toilet flushes. And the masts, he said, sticking out of the sidewalks with their wire rigging. The sewers full of them.

13

Joe, I'm back on the Condo tower. Trying to figure a way to pay the UK guy and my lawyer's fee. I sold the Pontiac for 800 US. Jail is gross down here — the food is drugged to make you sleep all the time. I go to court at the end of March and everything should be cleared up by April.

Daytona 500 was fantastic. I was trapped in the middle of 5000 RV's and it took 14 hours to make it 1 mile in the infield while the cars were doing 3 miles a minute around the circuit. On the photo you'll see four sparks behind the car. That's caused by a bump in the track. The steel plate that protects the oil pan hits the bump at around 130 mph. It's like your ribcage, Joe, protects your heart. The gas tank is your lungs — the car breathes on gas but you need oil to keep everything fed. Now Joe on this car after a hundred laps the steel plate wore through and he started leaking oil and before he could pitstop there was a slick three cars slid into and crashed. I didn't see it but I heard it and you knew who it was when they didn't make the turn. Strange waiting for them like that and then you forget them until you see a replay on a monitor. 3 day party I thought I was going to die with a hangover in the most expensive car park on earth.

14

I saw him on TV. I got it videotaped. I fastforward the race so that the cars are going a thousand kilometers an hour. He was sitting on the roof of his van at turn #4. I can press the pause button and hold him there. He's taking pictures as the cars pass. He's wearing the long-sleeved shirt our mother sent him. He needed large shirts to hide his arms. I'm not big enough for the Club, Joe. They're all on steroids and they're massive, see. If someone gets rowdy I got to wait until they're drunk and then I can take them. Once last summer he said Joe, does my nose ever hurt. From getting sunburnt? I asked. No, from getting hit. Funny how sometimes when he talked about her, he wouldn't say Mom, he'd say My mother. He forgot that we shared the same mother.

15

Dear Francis:
Happy Birthday! I hope it fits. If it doesn't
you can exchange it at Sears – but don't
tell them I've reinforced the buttonholes!
                    With love, Mom
                    X X X X X

16

They say he must have left some drawers open. They found wrenches and screwdrivers strewn all over, some almost a kilometer away.

When the van flipped he drove himself against the wheel so hard it left a blue arcing ridge across his ribs. Hanging there upside down his arms up like he was under arrest. A parachutist stuck in a tree. The weight of the tool boxes tore the floor out.

Physically, he looked fine. You would think a wrench might have got him in the head, a screwdriver taken out an eye. It was just that blue crush across his chest all caved in like that. The seat belt left a faint bruise across the blue like a Don't Smoke sign. Open casket.

Witnesses saw the van swerve. He held the front wheels straight but with the weight and the speed over the new tarmac, they use too much oil in the compound, he just slid over the surface. As the van turned it twisted over onto its side.

Scraped the road for a hundred meters. The driver's-side mirror was flattened smooth into the door. He had his window down and there must have been sparks. The van would have stayed that way if it hadn't been a turn. He would skid until friction stopped him. He'd climb out the passenger door, pat his hands and say Well that's that and start hitchhiking. But the turn came and he skated straight through the guardrail. The nose dug into a retaining wall and the van flipped onto its back. The floor caved in an hour later.

The police said he shouldn't have been driving on those tires. They were bald and undersized for the weight and he was lucky to have gotten this far. They didn't say anything about him running, that he was supposed to stay in the State and here he was in South Carolina. He was heading for Montreal, I know that. It was spring and he figured he could make the border before the call got out. It'd be warm enough in Montreal to get work and she might be there. He'd shag the lawyer and pay off Dad and keep the UK guy's money and stay in Canada. That was the plan all right, but the police never made anything of it. I guess they figured with him dead like that it'd be too much paperwork and for what purpose.

Introduced

■ ■ ■

The door is locked with an arm of wood that can be raised by a rope hidden in the eaves. It's my father's trick. You pull on the rope which lifts the brace. There's coiled rope and a hacksaw looped on a nail. Antlers over the fireplace. Boxes of matches stuffed behind a strut in the gable roof.

Dina is in the outhouse. From the back window I ask if there's toilet roll.

"It smells," she says, through the woods.

"There's twenty years down there."

The path to the outhouse is a blind curve, through the spruce, so our voices have no bodies. I hear Dina's feet drumming the tree roots that snake across the path.

The rugs are dusty. Kerosene lamps are empty. Candle holders show their prickets. "Just put the knapsack in there."

"Sleeping bag," she says.

My parents have put in a new window. There'd been rot in the sill. My father had chalked the dimensions of the new window on the logs, and then chainsawed the chalk marks. The mullions gone. Electrical cords run along the walls connecting light bulbs. There are little changes all over.

"We will need light," Dina says.

"I'll get kerosene."

The garden is partially harvested. There are still a few

drills of potatoes which a moose has slept in. The mould of its body has bedded down the plants. The corn is gone. Tomatoes still in the cold frame. A barrel for forcing rhubarb. Bushbeans, snowpeas. They will leave the cauliflower in the snow. Dig one up when they need it.

On the second acre a fire has chopped a gap in the woods. My father had been burning brush, and it had gotten away from him. From the road stretches a field of steel-blue trees. They cast long shadows which touch. We could have pulled the car right up to the cabin. Someone with a Caterpillar has torn a hole through the hill so you can see Pelley Pond. You can map the area with a glance.

Dina has found a few cans of food under a stainless steel bowl.

"We missed a moose." I explain the garden. "The thing ate the beetroot."

I turn the tap on the propane. The fridge door has been kept open with a piece of cardboard that was used as a shopping list. Lard. Tea. Milk evap. Sausage. 2 sliced. In my mother's hand. You have to keep the fridge open or mould grows. There's a package of wicks in the tinfoil drawer. We light three lamps and everything gets darker. "And water?"

I take two five-gallon buckets to the lake. I am not familiar with the new shoreline. The stepping stones are beached. I have to feel my way down.

Indian Lake is low since the pulpmill stopped tugging booms. The island separates sky from water. As I bend to dunk the second bucket there is a glint of eyes, I am sure they are eyes. Green. They are caught in a furtive moment and then are gone. There is no sound, just the eyes.

"There was something at the lake. Getting a drink."

"Something?"

"A lynx. A bear."

She is feeding kindling into the fireplace. I put my hand on the mantel.

"We made it on the floor. The chimney breast. We had it here, in a form. Then we lifted it. All the stones are from the beach."

"The sparkle ones are nice."

"Marble." My brother had found it on the island. You couldn't tell from the outside. You had to crack the rock to find the glint.

We had set the stones in cement. Once it cured we lifted it with levers. Dad knew it would crack. The two sides couldn't carry the weight through ninety degrees.

I hook the radio to the battery and we listen to short-wave. Americans are mobilizing in the Mediterranean.

"I am not used to animals," Dina says.

We sleep in my parents' bed. We peel away the sheets and slip in like insects. The sleeping bag is damp and our nipples are as stiff as rivets. We rub them together, laughing. Dina says "I know why you call the sleeping bag a knapsack. It is because it's a nap sack."

You can hear the generators' buzz from up the lake. A loon calls. The lake is cold silver.

The smallest of things can change a life. I met Dina Tumova's parents four months ago on St. George's Day. I was in Bulgaria. I was traveling through eastern Europe, writing columns for a Canadian paper. In Sofia I stayed with the parents of Ati, an émigré I had met before leaving. Ati sent me a letter. She wrote, "I know exactly where you are now. In a park opposite the British Embassy. I was in the Embassy where you picked up this letter. That is where I found information on Canada. I worked in the building behind you, in the Palace of Culture. Yellow paving stones. To your right is a grocer on the ground floor. He sells meat and bottles of nectar in a yellow window. My friend Dina wants you to visit her parents."

The Tumovas invited me to dinner. On St. George's they hang green leaves over the doorway. We ate in the piano room. They couldn't believe I was from St. John's, the city their daughter was now living in. That I recognized photos Dina had sent of herself standing beside a two meter snowdrift, of Dina entering a downtown cafe.

"Oh yes, I know that snowbank. I have sat behind that window."

I knew everything in the pictures except the person standing in them.

Ants nibbled the box of sugared apricots in the center of the table. Mrs Tumova sat on the piano stool. She wore a purple-striped dress. Mr Tumova had thin arms from a cancer. He wore a scarlet turtleneck, smoke-rimmed glasses and thick brown pants. I blew a fuse when I accidentally touched a light with my head.

We ate cold soup, lamb, roast potatoes, shopska salad. Mr Tumova offered a square of honeycomb from his apiary. The vegetables were from their ranch. They work from Friday night to Monday morning on their ranches. "We rest during the week." The ranch a half-acre allotment in the country.

When I returned to St. John's I arranged, through Ati, to meet Dina. She shared an apartment with another Bulgarian, a man she had met here. There was nothing decorative on the walls. Dina was moving to Montreal as soon as her Landed Immigrant Status was approved. I had done some interviews with Ati for the paper. The Human Rights board was on their side. Ati and Dina had been on their way to Cuba for a holiday. The plane had stopped to refuel in Gander. They got off with fifteen other Bulgarians.

Dina said, quietly, "We have to pretend we are being persecuted. That we are political refugees. But we come here for other reasons. There is no hope back there. It is messy and here we have choices."

I had brought photos. Dina stared at each one carefully. The ranch, her parents, the dog, the trams, her ex-husband and the Pirin dancers. Her eyes widened. She gave a quick shake of her head. "You are the only person here who knows my parents." I took out a small brown package from my coat pocket. "Here." Dina unwrapped the little jar. Honey from her father's apiary. Her red nails like bees.

I had met Dina's ex-husband. Ivailo had lost his job in the Department of Culture. He was applying for funding from the Kress Foundation. He did not like Dina leaving. "We were changing things and then she left. I knew she was going. Most of the young are going. Now there is no steam. No change."

Ivailo slept a lot. He showed me the gypsy corner of Sofia. Houses built from doors and flattened barrels.

I told Dina how her parents took Ivailo and me to the Palace of Culture. There was a concert. Mr Tumova clapped through the whole thing. The bones in his hands barely covered in skin. Men danced and played instruments while a phalanx of women jiggled frenetic limbs. Rouska Stoimenova sang rousing Macedonian nationalist songs. Whenever the gaida had a solo or the ukuleles hit a good groove the crowd understood. I bought a tape in the foyer.

We walked the Tumovas home. Ivailo invited me for coffee and a cigarette. We sat in a room with a TV and three couches. Ivailo had a tape player but he'd sold the speakers. He said "The songs were not portrayed authentically, but that is due to their Macedonian bias." Ivailo's uncle was there. He used to be a journalist. He said "You can print anything now, which means you get a lot of junk."

I'd gotten some mail from my parents and I showed them the newspaper clipping of the Indian Lake tugboat. The log cabin in the background.

To Dina: "You had written him long letters describing Newfoundland. He said you thought the houses were set far apart."

"And what did you think of Ivailo?" Dina asked.

"There was one afternoon," I recalled, "we were walking through a market. It was raining and people were peering into shoe shops to see if anything nice had arrived. I had bought a quart of strawberries for your parents. I offered one to Ivailo and he took it and ate it with indifference. But I could tell by the way he ate it that he loved strawberries and that he rarely ate them because they were so expensive."

"He still has pride."

"He said he thought I was generous but I said I was just being fair."

We sleep close because of the cold. In the morning I have forgotten the sparrow. A white-throated sparrow. Two-one, two-one-one-one. Twenty years fly by. Sleeping in the camper trailer. Waking to a green and orange canvas sky. The foldout wings holding parents, brother, sister. Cupboards filled with comics. The foundation of the cabin laid. Logs held together with ten-inch nails. Plumb line and spirit level.

Dina stirs powdered milk into water, pouring it on the cereal. She has made coffee in the aluminum percolator and toast on the bent clothes hanger. The cabin has never seen anyone like her. She looks faintly ridiculous against the logs. She is wearing earrings.

During our first meal she had said "I like men who are into their food. You must eat with all of your love."

The lake has a lop. Several jays screech from the tops of spruce. Dina is chewing a nicotine tablet.

"The jays are lovely."

"They peck out the eyes of rabbits."

"Really?"

"If they're in a snare. If they're dead. We had a trail going up past the Point. Up there. I'd sling the rabbits over my shoulder. They'd dribble pee on my coat. Sometimes, if we couldn't get out there, you'd find just the bones. Lynx if they're alive. Jays if they're dead."

"I would like to go up to that Point."

"There's cabins all the way now."

"You promised a canoe."

"It's under the floor."

We take the coffee out to the step. We squeeze together in the doorway. Along the path there are foxglove, loosestrife, monkshood. Pink, yellow and blue. A squirrel is chittering.

"You see the grass?"

"It is lumpy."

"When we first came that was trees. We cut a blaze from the road. We dug out the stumps. We'd go fishing, we'd bring worms from Corner Brook. We put this bit of grass in the tin to keep the worms fresh. After fishing, you'd come up here. Dig a heel in the ground and stamp in the grass. All that lawn is from worm tins. It's all bog underneath. Dried bog."

The jays are taking turns in the trees. I know they must have found something. "One night my sister swam to the island. She paddled over first with a tent and a sleeping bag. Then she swam over and stayed."

"She was not frightened?"

"She played her flute. We could hear it over the water: 'Early one Morning.' My father went down with a harmonica and sat on the big rock and played back to her. She'd start a song and he'd finish it."

"I think I will like your father."

Where the music met halfway across there's a large piece of bog. "It floats down slow. That bit used to be up by the Point, maybe six years ago."

"And this is that." Dina pats the ground.

We prepare the canoe. Paddles, lifejackets, a fishing rod. The anchor is concrete molded by a bleach bottle. I take the back and we carry the canoe to the beach. Dina is two steps into the sand when she sees the moose. She drops the front with a crack.

The carcass is bloated. Much of the hair has rubbed off the skin. The jays are perched, waiting. There is no smell, just the visual discrepancy. The beach, the water. Moose on the shore.

"It must have floated here. It's been dead a while."

The head half in the water. The eyes, nostrils, and the mouth are covered in fly specks. The antlers would have weighed the head down. They had dug in and the body swung around. The belly is swollen. Looking closer you can see where the bullet has crashed out of the neck. The blood clot is swarming with flies. There are maggots around the anus.

"Can we bury it?"

"We'd have to drag it in the woods. It'd have to be deep." Flies work at the sores.

"It is so large."

"It's too big."

I fetch a knife from under the stairs and saw into the flank. The meat is purply-red.

"We'll have to tow it."

We take the canoe to the edge. I fetch the rope from the shed. I tie a bowline knot around the front legs and neck.

Each time I nudge the moose a swirl rises. The flies are mad with the blood in the flesh.

"It is too much."

"It'll float. It floated here."

We tug it into the water. The flies lift and swarm. The antlers are broken.

I tie the rope to the back seat, leaving some slack so that the moose can float a few feet behind. We slide the canoe into the chop.

"Dig your paddle in and shove."

"It is too heavy."

"Just push, Dina. Let the water take the weight."

We have not decided where to go. Cabins puncture the treeline all the way up the shore. It's a mile to an empty beach.

"The island."

We head for the west side. Dina keeps banging her thumb on the gunnel.

"We'll go round the back. It'll float up behind, that's good."

Indian Lake is long, linked in a chain with several larger lakes. When we are clear of the shelter from the Point, the waves increase. When we are two-thirds of the way the wind is too strong. I have to steer and paddle.

Dina: "I don't want to do this anymore."

We have to shout over the slap of the canoe.

"If we let it off here it'll go straight back."

The wind has a lot of lake to work with. We paddle for ten more minutes, barely creeping forward.

"We'll have to leave it, Dina. Paddle to the island."

I cast off the rope. Without the drag we reach the island in minutes. Leaves of bulrushes flash on the shore. The bulrush cigars remain still. I turn a few big rocks over with my foot.

"Just a couple large ones. Two will do. They have to be flat, with a ridge."

I find a pair which are flat for the ropes. It's the marble in the fireplace. Dina rubs her thumb and rolls her shoulders. I place the stones carefully against the ribs of the canoe.

The moose has drifted close to the bog. Some boaters have tied bleach bottles to the bog.

"The rope. Don't lean. Get it with your paddle."

The waves are beating against the side of the canoe. I try to keep us into the wind. What should happen seems like common sense, but I'm not getting that. Dina passes back the wet rope and I try binding it to the biggest stone, but the stone keeps slipping out. "Throw the other one over, we won't need it." I lash the anchor to the hind legs.

From the shore the jays watch. I hold the stone and Dina holds the anchor. I count One Two Three and we throw the stone and anchor. The large thing beside the canoe goes under.

We wait. I can see it sinking. A few large bubbles bulge to the surface, then several streams rise like carbonation. The moose stops, just a few feet below the surface. You can see its form, almost standing. It has definitely stopped sinking.

"It's got to be deeper than that."

I push the paddle down, past the moose.

"It's stuck on something."

"Bog."

"Jesus."

Dina points her paddle at the bleach bottles.

She's sitting on the couch. With her thumb she's popping plastic bubbles in a sheet of packing insulation. Each one is like the crack of a knuckle.

"I can't stop thinking about it under there. It's stuck under a meter of water in a bog, with stones tied to it. Imagine finding that. Imagine your sister swimming into that."

"It'll rot. The fish'll have it gone. It's better that it's under water."

I had gone out back to plant some trees on the burn. I did six rows and they looked pathetic. Like puppies in a doghouse. They'll grow into the space. Millions of blueberries. It took six rows to get my temper down.

"Those flies," she said. "They were incredible. You have seen my father's bees?"

She quits popping bubbles to point at the ceiling.

"Once, I was in school and my friend said 'I think your father has gone silly.' We looked out the window and my father was staggering down the street. Pounding two pieces of pipe over his head. There was a storm of bees above him. He'd seen the bees, wild bees, and said to himself, I want them. He found the pipe and began to pound. He lured them into a tree. He found a box, emptied it. Found a stick. He climbed the tree and with the stick he stirred the bees like you stir jam. They swarmed around the stick and he put the stick in the box. Put the lid on. He took the box home and put them in the hive. I asked him if he was bitten and he said 'Of course.'"

"And now he's immune."

"He never wore the clothing."

She presses the branch of her clavicles with a thumb and middle finger, as if to hold down some great helium weight.

"He is so thin now. Only small things, from the inside."

Dina rubs her stomach. "I feel sick about the water."

It was only after we had come back and thought about boiling rice that we remembered the water. The dead moose and where I'd filled the buckets. We'd used about three gallons.

"It must have been a bear I saw. It didn't make a sound."

"What is a lynx?"

"It's a cat. They don't scavenge."

Dina is still concerned over the water. "You must have been very near."

The flies had been busy over a faint stain of blood in the sand. There was little else to show of the moose. The water in the bucket didn't look bad. I stroke her knee.

"We'll be in Corner Brook by noon. If we leave early."

"Your parents expect us then?"

We've tuned in to Voice of America. The announcer is confirming reports of military maneuvres in the Mediterranean. Somewhere there is a transition of power.

"They were introduced. Moose."

"What do you mean?"

She wants me to sit down, but something makes me stand.

"They're not native."

She brushes the soot on my jeans. "It's too bad about the fire. The place is so nice."

"It'll grow. The wind could have been the other way."

Creaking in Their Skins

■ ■ ■

Maybe I'm getting more sensitive. I've lived up north. Never as cold as last night. It was only what, four below. I walked Lynn to her car. We watched a man outside the bank take handfuls of salt from a bucket and sprinkle them over the sidewalk. His bare hand diving in for salt. In a thin shirt. The cold wind nothing to him. I got some money from the machine. Then I was walking to my truck. And my head where it's bald went numb, frozen. It was frozen. Never felt anything like it. I wanted to put my hands up there to warm it up. Run to the truck. But I didn't want to look foolish. I thought I was going to pass out, honestly.

And I've never worn hats. Hardhats on the job, that's all. I don't want to shock anyone. People who don't know me. I don't want people to think I'm trying to hide something. Everyone knows me here though, so it shouldn't matter.

Oh, I'd say seventeen. Sure, it bothered me at first. But then I said fuck the hair. Cut it short. Now I don't think about it. It's never been a problem. But I'll tell you one thing I've always been curious about: hair-dos. I love seeing what people got done with their hair. How they comb it. All the styles. If it's long or short. I'm fascinated with it, you know.

I fell asleep once and the kids drew a face on the top with markers. The hair in back was a beard. Pretty funny.

Anyway, when I got home I got a wool beanie and slung

it in the cab. Just in case. It was remarkable weather.

Lynn? Met her at a function. A big do actually. She played cello. The way her knees gripped the instrument, her hand on the neck like the back of a dance partner's head. Then a banquet. It was in honor of a building, the Fortis down on Water. We'd gone in with the seismograph to check the structure. Give the final go. And it was fine. So we were eating and the wine was no problem. We were all surprised at how much we were drinking. Lynn dropped her fork, leaned over to get it. She came up and said Excuse me, but my lips touched your cake. What was I supposed to say? I said it's fine. The first thing I ate was the impression of her mouth on the icing.

She had just moved into a house I used to live in. In fact she's got my room. Kim, who showed her the room — I said Kim still lives there — Kim said it was her room when she first moved in. Said a guy had left some stuff there for a few days. Me. One thing was an aquarium. No fish, just the box and water. The filter left on. Kim said it was there two nights and she couldn't sleep because of the noise. Lynn asked her why didn't she turn it off and Kim paused and said That's what I'm trying to alter. You see, Kim said, I never would have thought of that.

I've still got the aquarium, I told Lynn. And no fish. I like the plants and the flutter. The filter, well yes, you'd want it off at night.

At the dinner I took her hand and felt the line in my finger on her flesh. She held it up. I said I sliced it on a table saw. I was working at the trade school. This was my previous life. I was feeding the board and I couldn't take my finger off it. Done it a million times, just slide the plank against the guard, slip it along. Embarrassing with the students. But I couldn't get the finger off the wood. No pain. I was astonished by the blood. It flecked everyone like sawdust. Across the white aprons of the students. Over my visor. Then it was the finger and I fainted. They sewed it back on but it left a line. Even through the fingernail. When I clip it I have to do one side and then the other. When I got home the kids screamed. They saw the floppy sleeve of my jacket. Thought I'd lost an arm until they noticed the bulge on my chest, the white sling and my arm cradled there like a bottle of wine.

My wife was a woman most men could get along with. We knew each other from school, way back to first grade. We used to have competitions to see how faint we could write in our exercise books. Grade Ten my buddy Jimmy Parsons did the negotiations. On Friday nights we'd drag a couple of two-fours to North Star Cement. Climb down the sides of a sand pit, working your way down like a screw. We'd sit in there and the sound was short, deadened by the sand. We'd lie there like you were on the beach amongst dunes. The sand funneling up to the constellations. I said Jimmy, I don't want anyone else. So next night we were in Jimmy's rec room listening to his brother's stereo, man we were wrapped up in watts per channel and motorbikes. I had Paula on the couch. She had her shirt off and my dick between her breasts. She had big breasts. Her hair like a curtain closed on the show. A double crown. I kept pulling it up to see what was going on.

I was half bald then. I'd haul back my hair and see the corners receding. Freaked me out. But Paula never minded. She got pregnant with Jenny right after highschool, but it was more like a relief, I think. I mean we could get married then without any fuss. Moved out of my parents' place straight into an apartment up in the Heights. Right on the edge of town. You could see the newsprint ships coming into the bay. Even the tips of Blomidon mountains where we'd ski and drink vodka. Great sunsets. That first winter I caught rabbits on the other side of the road. We were that close to wilderness.

There were moose coming up for salt or just shaking the woods off their backs like they were glad to get out of there.

After Jenny we had Peter and I finished trade school. Two kids, a wife, a trade, and I'm twenty-two and dissatisfied. I love my kids. But it's a lot of work with a little bit of joy. Funny, recently I was looking at Lynn and she reminded me of someone. And then I saw that it was Jenny. Jenny said Waterlemon, and a butterfly slapping its wings. When I carried her on my shoulders she'd say My foot's gone dizzy. She had two ropes of my brown hair.

After having Peter, Paula got really fat. One day I noticed this lump on her jawbone. It was a mole. I said Paula, where did that come from. She said she'd always had it but I knew she hadn't. So she had to explain how it used to hide under her chin but now with the fat it had popped out and I knew right then that something had to change. I mean my never knowing it was there under her chin.

So we separated. I could talk about the fights, but to me the mole is it. If you want to hear the fights just marry someone expecting them never to change and you'll see what I mean. I was disappointed.

I built cabinets for ten years. I had a partner William Tiller, and his wife kept the books. We never seemed to make enough to pay the rent on the workshop. Router blades and stain. We bought tractor trailer loads of wood. We turned out some good product. Made banisters. We had a whole photo album of our stuff. But we couldn't keep it going. This franchise place with government subsidies moved in, so we declared bankruptcy. I snuck out a few beautiful lengths of oak. I got them up in my buddy Jimmy's rafters. I told him when I die I want that oak to go to Peter.

With the work gone I moved west. I went back to school and got hooked on engineering. I worked in Vancouver for a year. Up on those Spanish-looking anthill highrises. Putting in earthquake safety fittings and joists. On the seismograph you can see the guts of a building, what makes it stand, how long it can last. There are trees out on the islands that are two thousand years old. The roots go way down. There was a fire out there and they couldn't put it out. The fire lived in the roots. It spread underground. And they found this fungus — the largest living organism on earth — they found it tied to all these roots. It's like your skin being the largest organ.

A year and I missed the place. So I applied for MUN and bought a 1100 Harley with all the trimmings. The next step up is a helicopter. I drove that right across. Sometimes I'd take the helmet off and let the wind feather my head. I got a burn on my skull that peeled off like a sheet of plastic.

That's how I moved into the house Lynn is in now. I had to live with people again. Got the fish tank at an auction across the road. This old guy died and his folks don't live in town so they sold off all the bulky stuff. I used to watch him scrape his driveway down to the bone.

We walked from room to room. Everything tagged. The fish tank was in his bedroom, light on, the filter running ragged. No fish, and that appealed to me right off. Just the little green bottle with moss, the water fern and the colored gravel. I could see the old man in his bed watching the water circulate. I bet he even drank a few glassfuls, I know I do. Like a water cooler. Every now and then I'll draw off a glass and knock it back.

When Lynn stays over she likes to look at me through the glass, pretend I'm in there, floating around. And when she's got her face pressed to the glass I can see her reflected in the side panels, so there's three of her. Her six eyes darting around like round blue fish. "Change the channel," I'll say and she takes off her shirt. Presses her breasts to the glass until the nipples pop. Six nipples. Then I'll warm them up in my mouth. Feel the hair and the tiny mini-nipples puckering.

Occasionally she'll play. I have to keep the temperature steady and the humidifier on. I tell her about resonance, how it can fall bridges. How her notes are falling me. Her calves — I call them little cows — flexing under the weight of Bach. As she plays I kiss the small abrasions she's built up on the insides of her knees. Later she grips the hair around my ears and kisses the very top of my head. She says she can still see the face my kids drew.

At forty you can appreciate hearing those things.

Just recently I was walking home. It was the night after a sleetstorm. No hat. The gentle ping of the ice under my feet. My boots stiff as skates. I came in through the back way, across the field. Lynn was over. She had the blind down but you can still see through the slats. She was practicing. She had her hair down so it covered her face. It was after midnight and all the houses and trees were encased in a film of ice. The telephone wires creaking in their skins. The bedroom window was lit and the light seemed to leak around the edges, making the ice shell glow. Lynn was watching the black and white, the volume down like she usually has it, flickering a bright grey in the room behind.

I stood there a moment, perched to jump the fence. The frozen dogberries were scratching the siding. Then I bent down and ate some snow, watching the window through the pickets. Last year this time a flock of robins had descended to chew the berries off. From that window I counted fifty-six robins. The fermented berries left them intoxicated.

A sparrow through the banqueting hall in winter

■ ■ ■

I am looking for faults. Anything with a flaw. The utility of houses, the tolerance of pension checks, the sensibly-placed greenspaces and the carefully planned sewers and roads. I can't believe how uniformly decent everything seems. I am searching for cracks in the surfaces, for weeds thrusting out of the chests of walls, brittle concrete. When I discover these things I feel relieved.

I was camping with Janet in central Newfoundland. We were following an old map. A provincial park was marked on the map, but it had since been closed. We turned off anyway and followed the deeply split pavement. Grass like quivers of arrows shot in bunches two feet high out of cracks. And leaned over from the grade like a crowd waiting for a parade to approach. The car swished over the grass. The tips of overgrown alders scraped the doors. I drove slowly, as you do in a procession. Janet said It's comforting to know it doesn't take long for the earth to reclaim its surface.

I think about this as I walk up Dene Terrace. I am holding a copy of *Newcastle A to Z* which Hilda had loaned me. Each garden offers a rose bush. On the news in London I'd heard that all the wildflowers in Turkey were being dug up and sold. I remember seeing women arched on the hillsides, carving out bulbs like you'd gouge out the eyes of a potato. Turkish authorities were concerned. The bulbs are smuggled into the Netherlands, then resold as domestically grown.

As you pass each seriously-built maisonette you can compare the roses. There is little space, so the silent competition that exists between gardeners can only express itself through the single bush. It seemed settled that quantity of blossoms and height would be the determining factors. A few roses manage to extend themselves past the brick walls and to teeter nervously in front of living room windows, to be admired like kids on stilts.

At number 24 the rose bush differs in that there is only a single flower and it blazes out a solid fire-engine red. It makes you realize how subtle the others are, parading in connoisseur colors like Dutch pink, mikado yellow, and rose bengale. Because the brick row houses look identical, only the rose identifies the people inside. Instead of giving me the street number, Hilda should have said, Look for the bold red rose. I ring the bell. A short, smart woman answers.

Well come on in and give us a hug. I've only just got in meself.

The large warmth of her breast presses against me as she stretches tiptoe.

I thought you had a girlfriend.

She left early. She went back to Canada.

We were in Czechoslovakia. We had just checked Poste Restante in Prague. Janet's mother had forwarded her bursary application and the forms required for the fourth year social work program. We were sitting on a stone wall near St. Vitus Church. I need to get a job, she said. She had to get back to the life she was living. She asked if I was going too. An American had his video recorder pointed at us because something old stood behind us. She said I think two people stay together when they admire what the other person is doing. It's useful and serves a purpose. They are proud of each other. I want to do social work, it needs to be done. I don't know what you are doing.

I'm an optician, I said. It's a helping profession.

But you're not devoted, she said. You just fell into it.

She counted off the reasons on her fingers. She felt like she had to finish something and that I was choosing to do nothing except enjoy the luxury of being young. Traveling wasn't anything. I could tell that from the way she held the map. She could never tell direction from a map. She had to align map-north with real-north and then point in the direction we had to go. To me, that's not using a map. That shows you don't travel well. She got a flight in Prague. I told her to keep my boxes in the basement. That I'd collect them in a couple of months.

Joyce shows me the sitting room. She asks, You've been up to Shields? Did you get to where your Grandad worked? That's a canny walk. And the Balancing Eel, that was his pub. Norman liked his drink.

She's wearing a flowery skirt and blazer with a purple blouse. She doesn't look blind. Brass fireplace implements hang from the mantel. Several photos of dogs adorn the wall above. Windows flank us.

Now Hilda said you were just like your Mam, but I must say you sound awful Irish.

I explain that pockets of Newfoundland have Irish ancestry. The accents are similar. The owner of the optical store I'm in is Irish but you wouldn't know. I mention how folklorists come to Newfoundland to study the voice. I've seen them in Trepassey going door to door with a van-load of sound equipment. Comparing vowels to eighteenth century Dublin phonemes.

Joyce asks after my mother and I explain how she's retired.

That's nice. But she's only young. And your Dad's retired too. That wouldn't happen here.

I mention that he's still repairing TVs, VCRs and small appliances. That his pension is tiny and that he wants to set up a small business. My mother quit work because she realized if she had more time she could make the things she needs instead of buying them.

You did well to get out of here, Joyce says.

Joyce is my mother's cousin. During the war my mother lived in Castleview with Joyce's family. My mother had a school bag made out of blue cloth. She caught impetigo. She remembers picking bluebells on a hill behind Causeway Road. My mother hasn't seen Joyce since my grandfather, Norman, died nine years ago. We emigrated when I was five. She said Joyce was a great help at the funeral.

From the kitchen Joyce says, I was given a cake — I went to this opening for a new Wing at the hospital and the nurses pitched in. Princess Ann was there to cut the ribbon.

Through the hatch I can see her at the open fridge. There's no light on inside.

Well you can see it's a lot for just me and I had them eat half of it before I could carry it home on the bus. Being on Council has its merit. Would you like some whiskey? I think it's whiskey.

Joyce reaches for a wrapped bottle on top of the fridge. The paper is torn to the ribbon revealing a label. I tell her that it's Napoleon brandy.

Oh well, it's all the same, ain't it? No we'll save it. Just tea, righto, luv.

She orders me back to the sitting room.

You can bring in the cake and plates on that trolley, that's your help.

As I roll out the cake and plates I survey the room with a buyer's critical eye. I had expected to see more things ignored. Those things that require visual cues to assist in their maintenance. But the walls are well-painted, there are no stains in the green carpet, the moulding appears dust-free, and no stray objects hide menacingly under the bureau plinth. Perhaps she has someone in.

Now don't be looking at the garden.

She finds the trolley and plonks the teapot on it.

'Cause I don't have one.

Past the French windows six slabs of concrete neatly surface the backyard. I hadn't counted on this. I'd brought a gift.

I brought you seeds.

You what?

I brought you seeds from Greece. Mam said you liked flowers. I don't think she knew how bad your eyes were. It was no trouble.

I rattle some pods. The seeds sound dry. I tell her the plant husks looked rather exotic.

It was February. Janet and I had been splitting seed casings apart. On Karpathos, between Crete and Rhodes. We were alone for miles, walking a beach that had turned stony. We weren't speaking and I had been thinking too hard on how easy it would be to run her down and hit her skull with a boulder. How I could bury her in the stones and leave on a ferry to Rhodes and then Turkey. I'd write postcards saying we'd split up in Crete, that Janet was planning on returning to Canada. I think it would have been simple. We collected seed pods and hitched a ride back to the town. We were staying in a room with a large brocade on the wall of a moose marching through bulrushes. Janet made an arrangement in a wine decanter with the dried brown stems and rigid leaves. I made a chocolate fondue and we dipped dried figs. We made love with the last of our Canadian condoms.

I don't care to garden now, Joyce says. I grow a few herbs between the cracks. Thyme. They give off a lovely fragrance when you brush them with your foot. Poof, up comes the scent. When your Mam was over for Norman's funeral there were still some things in bloom. She went round inspecting. But what a tangle. You wouldn't believe the trouble I had with it. They were Ben's you see and I carried on for a few years, just for Ben, but I can't be bothered now. I have to cut out the things that don't matter.

It's obvious that Joyce has minimized the chance for accidents to occur. She has no stains in her carpet because she is very careful with her cup and saucer. She has eliminated the need to remove stains by preventing their occurrence. I study her sitting in her chair and understand she is not entirely comfortable with her teacup. She is used to having tea in the kitchen.

It reminds me of Benny, she says, when he came back on leave. He'd been stationed south, in Malta. He brought back a banana. Just one banana. I hadn't seen a banana in years. It had all gone brown. He didn't know enough to pick it green and that you shouldn't cover it up. But he said, Joyce, I want to plant it. I want to grow a banana plant in the greenhouse. We had a little one in the back made out of storm windows. So I told him, Benny, bananas don't have seeds. They've been bred out. You have to plant a bit of leaf. Well what a man, so sad. He could have had all the leaves he'd wanted but he took the banana.

Just how good are your eyes, I ask.

Well I can still read letters. I get a lot of letters, being on Council. I mean I read them on the machine. Here I'll show it off.

In the corner sits a black table with a large bright viewing screen. Joyce slides in a sheet of paper like you do at the library with microfiche film. The screen enlarges the text.

But I can hardly use that even. I need a secretary.

On the wall are two framed pictures of dogs. I look at them closer.

Nice dogs.

Yes. Now which one are you looking at? Oh the Lab, Ohma. He was the first. Beautiful dog. The other's Fay. I couldn't ask for better dogs.

You don't have one now?

Oh no. I've got me cane now.

Joyce reaches into her purse and pulls out what looks like a handful of short curtain rods.

It's collapsible. I can bring it anywhere, and I do go everywhere now that I'm over me nervous breakdown.

She says this as easily as 'headache'.

It was with me eyes getting worse and then Benny getting ill. He had cancer. And me daughter was to go to Oxford. Now I could've made a scene to get her to stay, but she would've hated me for it, wouldn't she?

She nods my way as if to say any young person would.

Taking care of her mother and her ill Dad. And you know the thing I'd hate most is for her children to grow up, hearing about us, seeing pictures, and thinking Aw, Grandma Stokle, she was the blind woman who lost her husband. Poor thing. Eeey that would kill me to hear that.

She pulls a long cigarette out of a vinyl glasses case and lights it expertly.

So my doctor recommended I go to Torquay, where they have the sighted dog training — you call them seeing eye dogs in Canada, don't you? Funny that. Well that's where I met Ohma. It was three months. Just touch and your listening. See I was still using me eyes and they were getting worse. I had to let go of them.

She flicks a thumbnail of ash onto her cake plate.

One thing I found difficult was having a fag. I'd get the wrong end in me mouth, try lighting the cork, and burn meself in the process. I still get confused when I'm offered one. I wind up singeing me eyebrows off.

The ashtray too would be in the kitchen to avoid carpet burns.

So you're an optician. Now you don't examine eyes.

No. I fit lenses.

It's not a difficult job, I tell her. I fill prescriptions, sell frames, cut lenses, do tint jobs. There's a lot of chemicals from the dye bath and fragments of glass from the grinder which hang in the air. I used to get headaches before the owner installed a couple of air ducts and a blower. There's a bead box for the frames. The dry heat expands the plastic and then you pop the lenses in. Customers complain that their glasses hurt. All they need is the nose pad adjusted or the ear piece molded. People are afraid to alter the shape of their glasses.

When I got back to Hebburn, she says, I had Ohma guiding. It was only then me friends realized how bad me eyes were. I was so used to getting around from memory. I got this interview for a job as a switchboard operator. Ben had me dressed proper and I was giving Ohma a brush when the phone rang.

Joyce inhales deeply on the last puff before screwing the butt into her plate.

The man apologized saying he'd have to cancel the

interview because the girls didn't want a dog in the office. Then me name came up for Council. And that's what made me run in the end. It was either that or feel sorry for meself.

She flips up the face of her watch and presses a button. A mechanized female voice says 4:25 pm.

I haven't let you have a word. I should've warned you that in Chambers I'm known as 'Joyce the Voice'. Now where have you been?

I'd walked to Shields market and took the path along the Tyne. Everything, I explain, looked meagre and reasonable.

There's not many ships now, are there? Ben used to work in the yard. That's what killed him. It's a pity your Uncle George isn't here. Factory Fortnight and everyone's off on their holidays.

And visited St. Paul's Church.

You were baptized in there, she says. Have you read any Bede? You'd like him. *History of the English Church and Its People*.

There was a bit at the Church, I tell her. A quote. Something like Life is the swift flight of a sparrow through a banqueting hall. The sparrow flies through one door of the hall and out through another. What occurs outside the hall, both before the sparrow enters the room and after it leaves, remains unknowable. It's a visual image, but Joyce sees it.

The oldest colored glass in Europe, she says. 1300 years. Bede had the best craftsmen in the world building that church.

The glass is a tiny circular window of faded red, blue and green. Across from it stands a bright multicolored panel with gothic arch.

You saw the new glass? The Princess of Wales opened it. Did I tell you when I met them, the Prince and Lady Di? It was right after I got into Council. This letter came. Ben brought it up to bed one morning with me tea and bacon sandwich — that's what I'd get him for his breakfast when he was working.

Joyce shakes her head and pulls at the weave in her nylons.

I can still smell them. I haven't had a bacon sandwich since he died, not that I wouldn't have one, mind. I don't think to make one for meself.

She stares at the front window, as if she can see the red rose just visible above the sill.

You know you'll get over her, she says. You're young.

And she leans over and presses my knee.

At any rate, up he comes wagging this letter by the corner, whispering It's got a Royal Seal. I'd been invited already to the National Sighted Dog Gathering and I figured it had to do with that. Princess Alexandria was officiating. So I let Ben read it. Me eyes weren't so bad then but it was a struggle. His fingers crinkled the paper. He says It's an invitation to the Royal Garden Party. Well I snatched it from him to read meself.

The Royal Garden Party, I kept saying between bites of bacon sandwich, reading the calligraphy with me loupe over me glasses, like a jeweller inspecting a diamond.

She laughs hard, slapping her thigh and raising a foot.

I told me doctor about it and whether I should go and leave Ben alone again after the Gathering. And all she said was You'll need a hat. And off we went and she bought us this huge red thing with a brim like a brolly. I got shoes too with these long spiky heels and Ohma had a ribbon for his harness.

She got handed in by this tall handsome fellow in a hat. Ohma controlling his urge to sniff the lot. The Garden is immense — two bands play at either end and neither interfere with the other. There are tents and tables with sandwiches and tea. She can smell the flower beds and the ivy walls are rustling.

The Queen and her mother are at one end and Prince Charles and Lady Di at the other. That's what I heard people saying. It was just four days to their wedding so I decided to get at their end.

And they gather into two lines when it happens: the rain pelts down. Buckets of it. Ohma sticks his head under the hem of Joyce's dress and those handsome fellows with the hats hand round umbrellas. Joyce doesn't need one at this point with her hat ruined, but it keeps the rest of her dry.

I thought for sure they'd cancel it, she says, but then a hush fell and you knew that Charles and Diana had arrived, hand in hand in all the rain, coming down a set of stairs from some huge French windows.

We held hands through most of Turkey. We bought rings in Marmaris. We felt closer out of necessity. It was like our last public performance. In the Kurdish southeast it was hard to get a room together. Our passport names didn't match. Janet was tired of meeting men. I can't talk to women, she said. I can't get close to them. Only the men will speak to you. The women hide away.

We kept touching each other intentionally. We shared a single bed.

Charles and Diana criss-cross to give everyone a fair chance to see them. We were on the grass and with the rain me heels sank into the sod. Lady Di was ahead of Charles because he loves to chat and she was still new at it. She crossed over and came right to Ohma. Ohma pulled his nose out and stood erect, puckering his eyes at the rain as Diana took me hand. She noticed the hat and said You like red too.

And here she was wearing red. So I said It's one of the few colors I can see well. She smiled and I wished her luck on Thursday, saying I hope it doesn't rain then. And the look she gave us was just like any bride. Oh no, she said anxiously, I hope not.

Snow is falling when we meet Ayhan. He is a Turkish English teacher who invites us to visit his town. You cannot say you have seen Turkey until you visit a Georgian community, he says. We'd gotten suntans in Greece and now, as I say, snow was falling. We travel by bus up through the northeast. The gravel pit hillsides turn into lush valleys. Green fingers of flowers thrust out of the soil. Men on the bus find our map curious. They handle it delicately, as if they are afraid their fingers might smudge the contour lines. Plastic Gypsy tents are pegged in fields. Children swing on ropes tied to forestry billboards. Şavşat is near the Iranian border. There are huge log homes which are used in summer when the sheep are in the hills. The people are poor. This is where Janet saw the women carving bulbs out of the hills. We are communist here, Ayhan boasts, pressing his closed fist to his chest. We drink beer with his comrades. Some have just been released from prison after a government amnesty. They all look fifteen years older than their age. This could be through neglect on their part: they don't count the years spent in prison.

Ayhan says Fascism ages us. We smoke hard and work at night like good communists ha ha. I must take precaution to stop people asking revealed question. I do not fast at Ramazan. I read banned books with covers of girls pasted. I make sure no-one can say I give communist belief to students.

Janet says her eyes are tired from the smoke and Ayhan replies with a serious face, We will hang those who dare to smoke. Later he tells us how difficult it is for a Turkish man to find a woman to love. He missed his chance with a woman and now he regrets. He grew up in Antioch where the people are mostly Arabic and atheist. The women don't wear scarves and the mosques are built by government order, not public demand. Janet asks if a woman has any choice in a man and he says Yes of course, but she cannot choose without being chosen. And a man must choose quickly.

Well I was telling everyone I'd spoken to Lady Di, right chuffed I was. The Queen had finished at her end so people were wandering down to get a glimpse of Charles and they were shoving us aside. So I said right loud You've had your turn, let us have ours. And he strode right over to where I was!

The Prince patted Ohmah. He asked Joyce if she'd come down for the Sighted Dogs Day. She said she had and that she'd been to Westminster to hear the Speaker of the House. The Speaker had been ever so nice saying the dogs were better behaved than most of his colleagues, standing when he stood and sitting after he sat. Charles asked if she could see him all right and Joyce said only half of him, meaning of course she could see his silhouette. I hope that half is my good side, he said and then added his 'better half' would be with him on Thursday.

We were on the Black Sea Coast when I asked Janet to marry me. I wasn't thinking straight and the environment was making me feel desperate. I knew then that Janet wanted to go home, that she was looking for a way out. I think when I asked her I only meant we'd be married for the time we were traveling. It wasn't a long term plan I had. I hadn't worked out how our lives would change. We'd been wearing rings long enough to make them feel comfortable. Everything in our knapsacks we shared. I saw myself in the clothes she wore. All our photographs have us in the same outfits. I said we could get married in Istanbul, wouldn't that be fun, or we could pick a small town and find the right officials. Maybe have a ceremony in a mosque. I wasn't think of what we'd be together once we were back in Canada.

Joyce marvels at her memory.

When I got back to Shields the councillors teased me for going. Like I've said we're mostly Labour. Thatcher never got her nose in up here. And they think we should chuck the Royals out.

Joyce pauses at this, wondering if she should have enjoyed herself.

Well I can't pretend I didn't, can I?

She checks her watch again and the voice states it is past five.

I'll have to be getting back.

Righto luv. It was lovely seeing you. Remember us to your Mam. We had a great laugh when she was over.

I lace my shoes. You've still got a rose in front, I say.

Oh, aye. That's Benny's too. Every year it comes back. It's nice having it when I come home from work.

At the open door she hands out the rest of the cake, wrapped in cling film. And then the bottle of Napoleon brandy.

Give it to Hilda. Jack'll have it for his tea.

She gazes down the road, smelling it.

You see those houses there. Well there used to be a pond we skated on when I was your age. Then a young girl fell through and drowned. They drained the pond and developed it.

When we first moved here, she says, there was only a path that the cows used. The mud they'd track up. Great ruts in the road. Now the floor trembles every time a bus passes.

75

In Crete we experienced our first earth tremor. The youth hostel in Sitia was closed because of the war in the Middle East. We arrived at night. I thought perhaps everyone was asleep. We found the door and it was padlocked. Around the back we discovered an open shutter. I crept through into a room with three pairs of bunkbeds. There was glass on the floor and the electricity was off. The mattresses smelled mouldy. Janet said There could be bugs. She was standing at the window in silhouette. A streetlamp carved the outline of her hair. The excitement of squatting wore off and we decided to find a hotel room.

That night the bed began to wobble, then the walls, and the whole earth felt legless. Lights blinked on through the town and distant screams floated through the air like voices over water.

By morning there had been three tremors. On the news in the taverna the weatherman circled the epicenter, 200 kilometers south of Sitia, deep in the Mediterranean.

As I walk down Dene Terrace I try to imagine the cow path running between the row housing, allowing walls to expand, freeing up more space for gardening. Beside the roses are peonies and snapdragons, day lilies and drumstick primulas. Even black currant bushes and a banana plant. The pond. All of this had been smothered by the two lanes of pavement, used rarely now except by buses.

They say life forms can live deep below the ocean, beyond the point light can penetrate. They survive the pressures, pressures strong enough to squeeze oxygen out of the water. They know nothing about light, about the worlds that exist above them. The life forms are blind and they live off the heat and oxygen escaping from thermal cracks in the ocean floor.

Flayed Man with Own Skin

■ ■ ■

I'll tell you how I met him. I was down at the Top and Bottom Club, me and Bill French. And Dave was serving at the bar. Now when I was working there you had to wear a tie and a clean shirt, pressed. You had to look smart. But Dave he didn't wear a tie. He had his shirt unbuttoned down to here and it was all creased. Now when I get a drink I'll leave a tip. But this feller was so ignorant, he didn't care, didn't want to talk to you, like he was above all that. So I made a point of waiting for my change, no matter if it was just a dime. But he didn't even blink at that. So I told Bill, I said Bill, this guy on bar is no good, where'd you get him? and Bill took me over and said Oh Dave Kelloway, yeah, he's a story.

We sat down and he told me how Dave and him and another feller went in partners on this bar that folded and Dave was the only one who got his money out, so now Bill's got him working at the Top and Bottom for nothing as a sort of compensation. No wage, just tips.

So when I knew this I felt like I had something then, like I was up on him. I went to the bar and asked him a few things, just to be pleasant, and Dave answered real ignorant still, but that was all right because I had something on him.

Then one day Dave was gone. Debt's paid off, Bill said. I found him later downtown. I said Dave, about the Club, and he said he'd finished up there and was opening a laundromat.

Bring your clothes down, he said, I'll give you a fair deal. I said, You might see me Dave, and next day I was there with this big whack of laundry and he threw it in the machines, dried it and folded it neat and said No charge for that. He got me curious, see. So I said fair enough and this went on a few times, same thing. Then one day when he was folding he asked me if I would move some stuff for him. I said Listen, I said, I'm not a garbage man I'm a mechanic. And mechanics make no less than twelve bucks an hour. Now for that I don't care what I do. And he smiled at me, first time, and showed me the backroom. What a hum. I want to put a row of video machines in, he said. But all there was then was garbage. Bags of it up to the ceiling and oozing out. He said it was a fish and chips before he moved in and the place was rotten.

I made fifteen trips to the dump. I had this stack there like my own personal dumping ground. One of the guys in the tractors came over and shook his head and I was just piling them on top of each other, flinging them ten feet high.

When that's done Dave says he's got some washers to move and a row of dryers. He's got a blueprint, this vertical view of the store and he had the space worked out, where to put the video machines. He was smart that way. And there seems to be a monopoly on video games in the city. Dave told me he bought the machines dirt cheap at an auction out of province and like they were the only ones he could lay his hands on to buy outright.

And it's funny the people who come in. All types of people. I thought like single mothers would use the place and you'd get the quarters off the kids. But man there's everyone. I mean people loaded come in. Some even have washers and dryers at home but they can't be bothered. And they all play videos. Like I'd never played them, but Dave gave me this returnable quarter that gives you a free game, so I started and are they ever interesting. Just how real some of them are. Like you're really shooting down planes or bombing cities. He's got one there you crawl into and the screen sort of wraps around you, so you're really there.

Anyway, up to that point it was all pretty much subdued. I hadn't put too much time into figuring him out. He's paying me under the table so it won't affect my claim. But then I get on at the garage and I can't do the work for him any more. We had a tarpaulin over the doorway to the backroom and we were going at it with crowbars and sanders, tearing the shit out of it. All the studs are rotten from a leak in the pipes. We tore it all out. And everything we put into it is good, but sec-ondhand sort of. Dave had it worked out, the cheapest way. But it's solid, nothing wrong with the way we built.

I got on at the garage then and I was doing odd bits of car-pentry for Dave on the side. He had a house he was renting too and he asked what I was paying a month and he shaved ten percent off that and I had the whole top floor. He came over to see how I was getting on, brought a case of beer as a housewarming. He saw me rubbing my back and said You're too tall to be a mechanic and I said I got to crouch under everything and he told me he could fix that if I wanted and I said It's right inside my back and he put me on the bed and gave me a couple of mean fists around the backbone, then sort of kneaded it and did it ever feel like he knew right where to push. So I asked him about it and he said he'd done three years of physiotherapy and knew all sorts about the body.

I told him I said it must be okay working on bodies, trying to fix muscles and stuff. At least you've got the same make of body every year. I mean we haven't changed in a couple thousand years. But a mechanic, he's got different cars every day. Fuel injection. Turbo engines. Anti-lock brakes. Computers. You can't keep up. That's why there's hardly any old mechanics. They give it up. I'm the oldest guy at the garage now, at thirty.

Dave said I was right about cars changing, but at least someone knows how they run. And you can get a manual on all the parts and figure out the relationship of everything. But the body, no-one knows for sure how it works. If you get hurt inside it could be any of a number of things. I said it's the same with cars. Mechanics spend half their time figuring out what's wrong. Even then they're not completely sure they're fixing the right thing.

We had a few more beers and then he asked if I knew where the garage washed the overalls. Like you know, fuck, I said. But I told him I could find out. So next day I told Roger Flynn I said Roger I know this guy who's got a laundromat he's interested in doing the overalls. And so I found out and the next week Dave had the contract. And the month after he's got all the franchises in town. Like there's six or seven. And it's all on the quiet, he doesn't tell me he's doing it. I see all these green uniforms from Eastend Garage and Westbrook Mall and he's hired on another girl to do the work.

And then one night I was over painting the ceiling and after we were through and rubbing the turps he says he'd like me to be his best man and would I do it. I didn't even know he was seeing anyone. So I said sure and then he says the wedding's in New Orleans, but I'll cover your way down. Mary's got a place for you. Just like that. He said he wanted her folks to see someone else from here, just to show we're normal people. And he's telling me all this like he'd talk about the shade of paint for the walls. What color will make people part with their quarters.

I got a week off work and he got the girls to manage the store. Mary had already gone down to prepare things. He found two cheap returns to Tampa and then we're on an overnight bus to New Orleans. The driver tells us over the intercom that federal law prohibits passengers from smoking tobacco, marijuana, or crack. That glass bottles are forbidden on the coach. That he hopes we're all comfortable and that he knows his voice is putting us to sleep. That at midnight, if anyone is still awake, he'll come down personally and rock us to sleep.

We got to New Orleans and Kate, that's a friend of Mary's parents, was offering a room at her bed and breakfast as a wedding present. That's where I stayed. Kate was having a family reunion herself and so I shared the bathroom with her daughter. It linked our rooms together. If you go in the bathroom you have to hook the chain on the other door. This is where things get interesting. Christine, her name was.

Now I haven't been with anyone since I broke up with Darlene. Like I haven't seen anyone. I mean that's two years, almost two and a half. And I don't know what you think about it, but like I don't masturbate. I think you shouldn't do that. It's not good for you. It's like you've got to think of someone else in your head to do it, I mean I've done it before. When I was younger. So I mean, two years. And she was next door. I could hear her on the toilet. And I'd met her, really pretty. Brown hair. Nice brown feet. Said she hadn't worn shoes in six months. There were these skin treatment tubes in the bathroom but I couldn't see what was wrong with her, if she had a skin problem.

I met the parents and the inlaws. Mary's parents. Dave's sister is down from Edmonton. Mary's got a bridesmaid, but it's a small wedding. The locals keep asking where Newfoundland is and what we all do up here and I tell them I live in the woods. I eat moose and I cut wood. That makes them think.

Dave's old man took us out to supper and then we go back to his hotel where the staff wear badges that say THIS IS A

DRUG FREE HOTEL and Dave says it means the employees have to take a blood test. Mr Kelloway, that's Dave's Dad, he's had a few and he pats me on the shoulder, sort of hauls me to him and says It's terrific you coming down all this way to see Dave. And they're living in Vancouver as if that's any closer. I had one from the cooler and then said I'd best be off.

I took a streetcar back to Kate's. Christine was playing guitar on the couch in a white t-shirt and cut-off jeans, barefoot still. She went really brown in the dark and she had little tits that sort of poked her t-shirt. She asked what songs I like because she couldn't think up any more. I thought of Darlene playing Cat Stevens. So I mentioned Cat and she strummed Father and Son and said You have to sing. I said I can't sing and she laughed and said she couldn't either.

The house is a big old one built off the ground because the city's below the sea and the Mississippi's got a levee. No subway. The trees all got roots over the ground because the soil's too wet. Any kind of wind will knock them down. The rooms are tall with transom vents and ceiling fans. The floors are cypress to stop the termites. Big palmetto bugs. A handkerchief garden in back.

Christine said she drove all the way from San Diego in three days. I said I'd once gone from Fort McMurray to North Sydney in four, but that didn't mean much to her. She said It must be hard being a mechanic up there with the weather and I said it depends on where you're working. Like where I am now at Westbrook it's fine because it's heated and they've got exhaust hoses in the garage doors. But like when I was working for Doug's Autobody — worked with the door open on a dirt floor. Ice going down your neck. No ramp. If you closed the doors you got carbon monoxide poisoning. Try taking a nut off with your fingers so numb you can't feel what you're touching.

Anyway, I went to bed after that. In the bathroom there was a blue nightgown slung over the towel rail. I heard her come in and thought I'd let her go first. When I thought she'd gone I tried the door but it was still latched and I said Sorry, and she said That's okay. Then when she was done she said I'm finished and I went in and saw her door closed and the nightgown gone and did I ever want to just twist the handle and go in. There was hair in the tub, gingery and kind of straight for being what they are. I squeezed out a crap, trying to be quiet, and I washed my dick in the sink just in case. Don't laugh. And I just lay there on my bed with the fan whirring, hoping. But nothing.

I had breakfast with her and Kate. Bob the brother was watching things Kate had taped for him off the TV. It sounded violent, being breakfast. Christine had her hair back. She said she was going canoeing with Bob and his wife probably the day after the wedding and would I like to go because they had two canoes. Bayou country. I said I'd check with Dave, but sure it sounded fine.

I met up with him and Mary in the French Quarter. Mary's a nice catch. She keeps in shape and she laughs good-natured at your jokes. But you can see there's something bigger going on between her and Dave. You can tell they've got a big love. Dave asked how the room was and I said it was fine. He said I'm thinking of staying there tonight. He wanted to be away from his parents, night before his wedding and all. I figured I'd take his place at the hotel but he said we could share the bed if the bed's big enough. I said Sure. Big bed.

So that night I asked him if he wanted to go out for a drink, like I know the best man is in charge of the tear, but I figured Dave wasn't into that. But he said he wouldn't mind a beer at this point in life, so Christine showed us this little bar on the corner of Camp and something, this shack in the middle of a residential area, and J.D. and the Jammers were getting blue. J.D. playing a mean harp. He had an empty mineral water barrel beside him and after each number he'd thank the band and ask the crowd to Give it up one time for Mr. Kent Wood. We couldn't figure out who Kent Wood was until Dave noticed people poking bills into the mouth of the barrel. The brand-name was Kentwood water. We gave it up one time and headed back to Kate's down this straight road of houses and those big fucking magnolias.

Dave said he'd driven over this bridge today and the bridge is the longest in the world and he said they stopped at phone booth 156 which is about middle way and he said you couldn't see either shore. The bridge was so long the earth fell away before you could see the end and all there was was this road over water with no land in sight. Sort of like the prairies, he said, the road so straight but just water below you. Kind of spooky.

He checked the bed and said Hope you don't mind, and I said no, it'll be like sleeping with my brother. He used to climb up into the top bunk with me. I told Dave how the bathroom worked and how I was going canoeing with them on Sunday, maybe see an alligator, and he said I was doing all right.

I was rubbing my back again and he said he could fix it and he did. Gave it that pressure. Then he took this book out of his suitcase. Big book. He said he liked to keep his hand in on the physiotherapy stuff. We sat on the bed with the spine between us. All these drawings of the body. A history of anatomy. The skeleton and stuff was easy enough because they could dig up dead people for that. But if you wanted to figure out muscles and nerves and tendons and ligaments, well you had to dissect and do autopsies. Some of the drawings were called Muscle Man, just muscles standing as if they were alive, no bones, with strips of skin peeling away at the elbows and kneecaps. Parts were labeled a, b, and c and there's usually a backdrop of a rhinoceros or a town hall or tombstones.

There was one of a man peeling the skin away from his stomach with his teeth to show the intestines. And another was called Flayed Man with Own Skin. Look, he gave me a copy. 1556 and that's just a photocopy. He's all muscle, see, and in one hand he's got a dagger and with the other he's holding the sheet of his skin with a ghostly face. The guy who did this one worked with Michelangelo, Dave said, and he was doing a play on some work he had to do for old Mick.

I put the fan on, and we crawled in, me by the wall. I could hear him thinking, I swear. He was looking straight up at the blades of the fan. I said Where're you going for a honeymoon and he said they were taking her parents' car and going down to Mexico. I said You ever been down that way before? and he said he'd spent a month in Nicaragua and mentioned this guy Sandino, who sounds decent. I said How long you figure you're gone? and he said two weeks maybe and I said I guess I won't be paying next month's rent on the first and he said they were moving in below me and he expected the floors to be sanded and varnished by then. I guess tonight we'll see if we'll be good housemates, I said, and he said I hope you have light feet. I asked him how he thought the girls were doing at the store and he said he wouldn't be surprised if it was a Chinese restaurant and I said It's sort of hard to believe in the life you leave behind and he said that's half the reason I brought you down here.

The shower went on and I told him that's Christine. You could tell from the way the water wavered which parts of the body she was on. It hit the curtain and you knew she'd bent over to soap a foot. She started humming and I said She can't sing, Dave. He said You're thirty right? and I said I was and he said The body stops growing at twenty-five. Everything, he said, that's built is done by then. Your bones have fused. All your body does is replace cells. Repair tissue. There's nothing new after twenty-five. Except, he said, the bones in the skull. They never completely fuse. There's always room for them to float around a bit. Some people even have a soft spot where the bones don't quite meet. He said if he ever goes bald he's going to have some bony head.

We lay there. Staring at the ceiling. The fan whirring. And Christine in the shower. And the condensation on the window was on the other side of the glass. Air conditioning, see. And I thought This is as close as we'll ever get. Here tonight. Close as I've ever been to anyone, really. I mean he was all there. And I felt his finger. I had my hand down by my leg and his hand came over slow and he put it on mine. He took my hand and held it firm and said, Sometimes you're far enough in you're on your way back. And I knew exactly what he was looking like as he said it. That deadpan sort of look so that you couldn't take him holding my hand any sort of way except a man being close to a man. And I realized I'd been tight in bed. I'd been worried I might brush up on him during the night. But that one touch, that deliberate thing made it all comfortable.

Growing Old

■ ■ ■

Instead of Hello he was answering with Merry Christmas.

A light voice said "I'm calling on behalf of Mr Albert Kenney." The line felt local, but it was all the way from Burnaby, B.C. Phil could hear Albert coughing behind the woman. The checkered shirt. The cap. Albert.

The nurse said the Clearwater Home was looking for a twin agency in Newfoundland to organize a walkathon. She said they had written Phil's Chamber of Commerce. No luck. "Then Mr Kenney gave us your number."

They wanted the address of an Old Folks' Home in St. John's. A map of the city. The whole time Albert's coughing. The beard. The boots with rubber straps to hold his oilskins. All there in that cough.

Phil said he'd send a map and make an enquiry.

Phil's wife said "Who was that?"

"Albert," Phil said. "He's in B.C."

Albert had been a neighbor in Trepassey, just south of here. That was five years ago. Phil and Mary out of university, taking care of a friend's house over the winter. If they kept the place warm and the kids from beating out the windows. Albert next door. When the pipes froze he let Phil carry buckets from his kitchen. The walls jammed with Holy pictures. Frames touching. Albert's wife had died. His sons had

87

moved to British Columbia. All of them, directly. As if they needed an ocean, but not the Atlantic.

"You remember when he asked if we were married?"

Phil looks at his wife. "I can't say."

"He asked me privately and I said yes and then he asked you and you said yes too even though we weren't."

"And then we figured we must have been."

They remember the moment and the feeling they had then for each other.

"Call the Hoyles Home," Phil's wife says.

Phil and Mary get calls for the Hoyles Home twice a week. Their numbers are one off. When Phil says "Hello," there's a pause and then, "Is this the Hoyles Home?" A few hang on. "Gerry's not there, is he?" So Phil puts on Gerry. Sometimes Mary does it, but she can't do it as well as Phil. He can get into it. Once, Phil spoke to a woman for an hour. In an old voice, he was the woman's eldest brother. He left her feeling happy. That her brother felt no resentment. He didn't want to be in the way, under her feet. He preferred his independence.

Mary tapped the number. One off. The desk said that Phil best come in and talk to Ms Avery.

"I don't have time to go trudging in to Ms Avery."

"Oh, what are you doing. It can't be far."

Mary got out the street map and it was far. One off the number, but far.

"I'll find a bus for you," Mary said.

Phil said "Where did we get this map? I have to send a map."

"You take Route 14," she said.

She was keen on seeing this through.

That night, in bed, Mary said: "I'm thirty, Phil. I'll be thirty-one."

It was a feeling she'd been having all year.

"I'm just not sure," he said back.

"You're never sure until you have one."

"But how would it be."

"You'll get work. I can get leave," she said. She stroked the hair on his leg.

Mary worked at City Planning. She'd been with the City for three years, promoted twice. It was enough to keep them both.

"I'm just not sure," he said.

After she drifted off Phil got up and watched the late movie. There was a doctor drugging his patients. During the commercials Phil wrote a letter to his parents. At three he turned in. He felt the duvet for Mary, to see what side she was on. As the room grew lighter he watched her eyelids flutter. She could never remember her dreams, but Phil often found her having them.

A dream he used to have frequently. A revolving cube inside his head. It would expand until he felt too close and had to push away. Grow again. Push away. Until it seemed everything was in that cube. Moving towards him, cramming his brain. It would crush him if it got too close. Then he'd wake up, sweating and tense, and realize he was fooled by a fabrication.

He pressed Mary's earlobe. He felt the scar tissue surrounding the pierced skin and shuddered.

Phil traded feet as he waited for the bus. A cold snap had moved in overnight. Snow had melted then refrozen, leaving a crust of dirt on everything. A finger of dog shit lay stiff near the bus stop pole. The pavement stretched over the hill past the house and down into a belief that it continued on for the mile to the outskirts. The City had tied holly to the lampposts. Phil watched an old black Lab make its way over the crust. The dog was thin, his backside worn like a shoebrush. The Lab sniffed the finger, nudged it from the crust, and with one short lunge of its jaws, crunched and swallowed it.

Number 14 stopped and Phil checked. Yes, the Hoyles Home. The pneumatic door wheezed shut. Several women on board discussed the Home, and Phil wondered if he'd ever spoken to them on the phone.

Ms Avery was around fifty, with a wide, sensible face. She said it was hard enough as it was. The activities, the swimming, arranging a charter. There was bingo and the movies at the mall. And now the tree and decorations. Everyone gets a garland. "I can't see a walkathon. Do they mean now?" She showed Phil the snowbank eating at her window. "The supervision. The city's a big place."

"Are you married, Ms Avery?"

Ms Avery didn't know what to say.

"I just wanted to know. I'm sorry."

Phil gave her Albert's name, the nurse, and the number in B.C. It was all he could do.

A reminiscence class in one of the rooms. Social work students had come with objects. Phil leaned in the doorway. A woman in her nineties grabbed a carrot. "A raw carrot," she said, holding it tightly with both hands. Then tears. "I haven't touched a raw carrot in thirty years."

In the hallway a group of carolers were banging snow off their boots. Phil thought he'd hang around. He followed them to the dining hall and they sang in front of the closed buffet. Their throats loud with song while Phil spoke the words gently, below what his ear could hear. Amongst the elderly were several faces of men and women not much older than Phil. Their youth stung him.

They did 'We Three Kings' and 'Silent Night'. Slowly the carols returned. They knew several verses. Then a resident walked over to the TV, which had been left on, and cranked up the volume.

There was instant coffee. A woman in her eighties rolled up to Phil. She knew him, his mother and father.

"I used to take you to Sunday School," she said.

"Mrs Hewlett."

"Oh, I'll never forget that Passion. You played the shepherd. You lost your flock and you cried, we couldn't stop you."

She lived next door to Phil's parents. Her hair was short, almost to the scalp. In fact you could see her scalp. The hair rooted like a doll's. Her skin puffed and white. The wheelchair inching back and forth under her hands.

"I was in a commercial," Mrs Hewlett said. "They needed a mature lady in a drug store."

A bad heart had taken Mr Hewlett, she said. She came out here to be with her kids. But then they left the province for work. Josh and Julie in Alberta and Ontario. Josh had married again, had a baby girl Mrs Hewlett had never seen. There was nothing left for her but here.

Phil said Mr Hewlett had been lucky to have her.

"Oh no he wasn't. If it wasn't me he would have had someone else."

Phil told her he had married a woman from town. No, no kids.

"You come by any time," she said.

Then he walked home. The snow under his feet like the twist of rubber. He remembered the Christmas the Hewletts' poodle died. Phil was over with a present from his mother and suddenly wondered what they had done with the corpse. "We put him in the freezer," Mr Hewlett said. "Come, I'll show you."

In the deep freeze, beside the frozen cod and steaks. A clear plastic bag with the black fur back. "We'll bury him when the frost goes."

On the way home Phil checked a used clothing store. All the pants he liked had 42 waist. He mailed his parents' letter. On the back he mentioned Mrs Hewlett. He picked up a few groceries at a family-run superette. Ms McGrath ran the cash and she was called Ms McGrath by all the staff, even by Betty, a woman much older. Betty sometimes wore a terrycloth bathrobe under her coat. Most of the customers were over fifty.

At times Ms McGrath would have to go in the back and Betty would guard the cash. She'd look at you and say "I don't know what Ms McGrath could be up to." Then she'd look at the black cash register and finger the wooden cash box. And then Ms McGrath would appear and say "Betty you know how to run the cash." But Betty would only bag.

A retarded man sang 'Jingle Bells' at the door and ran on the spot as they went dashing through the snow. His red cheeks had grey sideburns and Phil thought he must be the oldest retarded person he'd ever seen.

A fat man sat arms crossed on a bench outside the superette. He was wearing a curling jacket with leather sleeves and across one arm was Bernadette. The bench made of wood painted green. Near the fat man a small grey maple stood leafless in a box of concrete. The bench and the tree, along with the black lamppost just to the left of the fat man, were all part of the city's scheme to revitalize the downtown. Phil nodded to the man and sat next to him. He recalled Mary describing the blueprints of what the city would look like in thirty years. Phil tried to imagine himself at sixty-five, walking through the blueprints.

In a second story window that looked back on to the

street, Phil could see a woman's head. The woman was fiddling with something, then steam rose and her head turned towards the window. It was Mary. Phil was shocked that their window was not made of ground glass. He wondered if she could see him. She lifted an arm, elbow over her head. She took a bar of soap and washed her armpits, looking into them as if expecting great clumps of dirt to be rinsed out. This is my wife, Phil thought. This is who I have.

Then she was slowly erased by condensation.

"You live there," the fat man said. "You order pizza from Venice."

Phil picked up his groceries.

In the basement apartment next to his house he saw three men at a green card table. The green reminded Phil of a chunk of golf course. It was peaceful as he often thought golf courses were, although he'd never been on one. He realized then a golf course was something he'd seen only on TV.

On the radiator lay a letter addressed to him. Mary called, "Is that you?"

Phil put down the groceries, hesitated, then took the stairs. He bounded up to the bathroom. He took off a glove and reached in to grab her at the hip.

"You're freezing!"

He put the back of his fingers on her neck. Then he climbed up onto the bathtub. He made a little circle in the steam and stared back at the fat man.

"It's me," he said.

Zero Hour

■ ■ ■

The seats are high with hydraulic shocks, so it's like riding a waterbed. Soft as a mushroom. Manny shifts gears, leaning over to check my mirror. Written in white: Objects are closer than they appear. On the dash a color picture of a child, maybe five years old. There are hands around the waist of the child, but whoever is holding her from behind has been chopped off. Just the hands are there.

"That's my daughter," Manny says.

"She's pretty."

The photograph is damaged in areas, as if it had gotten wet and stuck to the glass in the frame and then been pulled off. Little bits are blurred where the chemicals mixed.

"You come from Toronto today?"

I tell him that I slept outside of Montreal last night.

This old Italian had brought me in to Montreal. Took me up the mountain, all the lights. He bought me six subs and a couple cans of coke. He was going to take me home in the suburbs but he called his wife. She changed his mind. He runs a construction business and she takes care of these chickens. He dropped me off on Route 20 near a Honda plant. New turf laid and the sprinklers on. Floodlights lit up circles of wet grass. I had to walk back to a drive-in Cinoplex. Crickets were grinding. Hard grass. Ground was rough like farmland. Ate a sub and watched a movie on the screen in the distance. This big picture hanging in the air with no sound. It looked like a loud movie.

"You a student?" Manny asks.

"An archaeologist." I was returning from a dig in England. Wookey Hole.

"So you going home?"

I had a job down in Port au Choix. "I couldn't get a flight back to Newfoundland," I tell him. "They never heard of it. Had to go to Toronto. Actually, we did land in St. John's, right where I wanted. Ever good to see those trees. You know the land is pretty wet when you're in the air. But they wouldn't let me off. Refuelling, she said. They weren't letting anyone off. Too many defections. We flew right over the house."

"They wouldn't let you off."

I'd never been to Toronto. Where Zuza lives. I hadn't seen her since a dig in Greece. I called her from the airport. Wenxiong answered. Then Zuza listed the subway stations to take. Same as London.

"So you dig up bones and stuff," Manny says.

I say that's part of it.

"Well I don't know about that. The wife used to talk about that. Like, I got no problem with the evolution. But she'd say they never found a giraffe with a short neck. You know what I'm saying? Like she'd say 'there's variety and there always was.' I mean she thought the star of Bethlehem was put there by the devil. I'd come home and she'd say those wise men were out to get Jesus. She'd have the Christmas tree flung on the lawn."

About the bones we found in Port au Choix. It's a burial ground for Maritime Archaic Indians. It cuts through Mrs Scanlon's backyard. I worked on the site last summer, stayed at Mrs Scanlon's. We found ninety graves, half are children's. The deeper you dig the older you get. But I don't know giraffes.

Let me describe Zuza. Her shoulders dusted in freckles. Two small scars the size of apple seeds on her cheekbones. She was with a Portuguese guy, on a bike tour around Europe. I was digging irrigation ditches in Crete. We met in Giorgio's Taverna. We played Scrabble on a miniature magnetic board. Zuza asked if there was any more work and I got her on. She was leaving the Portuguese.

"I love his voice, his family. But he bites his fingers and he can't decide on anything."

We drank krassi while a TV played Hollywood movies dubbed in Greek. There was a stuffed vulture in the rafters. A clock with just a second hand. Giorgio said it measures time instead of telling it. Men were toasting bread on the woodstove. Zuza was writing the man she's with now, a Chinese neuroscientist. "You will be our first guest," Wenxiong said when I got to Toronto. When shone. Heard about him in Greece three years ago and there he was.

Zuza with straight black hair. Long arms. A swimmer's body. Her parents are from Bratislava. Emigrated when she was five. Zuza dug harder than most of the men. We counted blisters from the mattock. I had twenty-two on one hand. You could hear the sheep in the hills. The tough soil we turned grew dry in seconds.

The crew ate at Giorgio's. One night there was a thunderstorm. Big white claps above the taverna. The lights went out. Everyone gathered at the windows, glad to be in. But the two of us shared a reckless look.

The Portuguese knew it was over.

We snuck out into the storm. Ducked under a stand of dark olive trees with nets on the ground. A few sheep huddled near a wire fence, clanging. The legs on one side hobbled, so they wouldn't bolt. The lightning flashed views of the fields and the Mediterranean below. You could see the lines of white caps driving for the shore. The Graeae. There was no space between the light and the thunder. Everything was immediate. We held hands, nervous, our blisters touching. We felt our hands like blind people do. Zuza had someone at home and I pretended I did too. She said I was the first person she'd ever seriously thought of besides Wenxiong and I had the same thing to say. I wanted to be on the same footing. She held my shoulder blades. She said that in Slovak they are called 'little shovels'. We touched noses, foreheads, and kissed lightly with rain on our lips.

In Toronto I slept on the futon. Zuza is a reporter for the Toronto *Sun*. She was covering that Kayla case. It was in all the newspapers when I landed. Every bus stop had a color poster of Kayla in a happy time. Then a second photo with Age Progression. Kayla is holding several trout. Their gills threaded over a forked stick. Zuza saw the child's body at the harbor. The ambulance and the plastic bag. She had to stake out Kayla's parents' home to see how they looked if they went outside.

I am five hours ahead. Their apartment has no plants. The kitchen looks out onto the fire escapes that spiral down the doughnut-hole center of the apartment block. A patch of sky filters down the shaft. You can watch the elbows, backs of people manoeuvring around their kitchens. Wenxiong and Zuza call this Channel One. They watch the windows, annotating their neighbors' stories. "Val and Luis want a baby. The Marmelos are splitting up. When Mr Okri leaves, his wife has someone in. Look, he's having coffee, kissing her right there." The living room window is Channel Two. Here you can watch several Chinese women perform Tai Chi. The fire escapes twist like a cord of DNA.

I read thick spines on the bookcase: *Principles of Neural Development, A Brief Atlas of Histology, The World of the Cell*, and

From Neuron to Brain. There are drawings of tiny things. Photographs of the interior of a cockroach leg. Wenxiong has been studying cockroaches, placing cantilevers on their legs to measure strength and reflexes. His results have had a practical application that deals with torque. But he's developed an allergic reaction. "Nobody eats cockroaches," he says. He's had to switch to rats. He is putting stress on pregnant rats. That fools up something and all the male babies will want to go with other males. Wenxiong is exploring the link between stress and sexual preference.

In the morning Wenxiong wears a velvet robe. The robe with light splotches on one flank from spilled bleach. For breakfast they make boiled rice balls with lotus flower seeds and another flower inside. Chewy, then your tongue dissolves the powder.

I dry the dishes. Zuza hands me a knife. The meat of my index finger surrounds the blade. It draws blood.

Zuza grabs my hand, runs the finger under cold water. She is holding my wrist as you would a child's.

Wenxiong has a box of bandages. "Sharp," he says.

Zuza is holding my palm where the blisters would be.

Wenxiong applies the gauze and tape. He tells us of a man in Shanghai who was hungry. Maybe it was his father. He goes into a bakery and strikes up a conversation. The man, his father, draws pictures on the counter with a finger. The finger is full of sesame seeds that have fallen off the bread. He puts the finger in his mouth. There is one sesame seed he cannot pick up. So he pretends to think about a point, then pounds the counter with his fist. 'Ah so!' he says and the seed pops into his mouth.

I flex the finger and feel the new edges of flesh rubbing.

Zuza wants to know if a myth builds around someone after three years. I say you tend to condense things. Put all of the action into one moment. You forget about the distance in between things. When you're confronted with the person, events tend to slow down.

Wenxiong describes the kinds of heavy metals they pour down the sink. At work there are rigid guidelines for the disposal of thousands of millicuries, but the drain is there. "It is so tempting. The sink is such an easy thing. It cuts out a lot of procedure."

He works with nasty people. One man, each time he cuts off the head of a rat, he says "Bitch." Another ends his sentences with "fuck," as in, "How are you doing, fuck?" Wenxiong is convinced that if you are nice and have charisma you will get everything.

They speak Mandarin when I am not in. I hear bits when I am outside the door. Zuza using a higher voice. When it's cold she wraps a wide scarf around her hips. "It keeps my vitals warm." She says they don't use much English. They discuss international borders. I am surprised at their tolerance for the Chinese government. Burma is British and Vietnam is French. Tibet is not a clear case of invasion. Korea was always a satellite until the Japanese conquered it.

I am there three days before I realize I haven't seen either of them outside the apartment.

Zuza at the newspaper and Wenxiong putters around, tapping on the computer. Occasionally going to the lab. On purpose I go to Kensington market with him. I describe to Manny how Wenxiong had to talk English to this shopkeeper because the man spoke Cantonese.

Manny grips the wheel tight. He guides the gear stick. Pushes the clutch. He shoves a tape into the cassette player. The cassette box advertises 20 Golden Country. We pass a large gathering of cars, people with sleeves rolled up. There are prefab building materials lying beside a grey concrete foundation.

"Jehovah's Witness. They're putting up a hall this week-end."

A side is being hoisted into place.

"So you don't think there's a God, Manny."

"I don't believe in one, not the way Norma does. "

"That's brave."

"My mother was a strong woman," Manny says. "She had faith like that. Hard faith. But her last words were 'I'm afraid'. Now my sister, she had no religion. She lived her life with no regrets. Lived to the fullest. Then she got a cancer down low. And she said 'It's alright if I go, I don't mind.' Now you tell me who's the braver."

The army on the road. Manny cruises in behind a convoy of military vehicles. The Jeep in back has a crew wearing fatigues and shades. They stare at us as if we're the only thing worth staring at. Manny creeps up on the Jeep so we're right over them, looking down. They keep the pace at a steady eighty clicks and never try moving over to the shoulder. "Ain't that special," Manny says.

I ask him what he's hauling and he has eight tons of con-struction boots.

"I used to haul for Pizza Delight," he says. "Had my own rig — one of the few Independents left. You make a little more, but it's a lot up front. A rig like this is a hundred thou-sand. You make a dollar twenty a kilometer instead of a dollar fifteen a mile. I drive three thousand kilometers a week. Costs run a dollar five a mile so you don't make much. Some-times I'd haul fish tubs back from St. John's."

He nods my way.

"I'd phone ahead from Clarenville to see if I should get

there with an empty truck. That was extra on top of the Pizza Delight contract."

"That's alright."

"Insurance is bad. One accident and the rates go up. I had to sell. Trying to miss this deer I went in the ditch. Jack-knifed. Had a concussion for three weeks. Lost my teeth."

He brushes his front row.

"Try to get insured then? So I work for Big Wheel. Sometimes there's product left over at the end of a run. I'd go to Marystown with twenty cases of bologna. I'd ask the foreman at the fishplant to put it over the intercom. Twenty-five bucks a case for five big bologna. In ten minutes I'd have it sold. Palettes of cheese. I still got soup left after one job."

"That's where I grew up," I tell him. "Marystown."

Another trucker pulls up in our draft. Bunny Wheeler. His windjammer is a set of plastic rabbit ears. Manny puts the CB to his mouth. "What kind of rig you got there?"

Bunny describes the engine size.

"Well, yeah," says Manny, "okay it's got a motor, but what I'm asking is what sort of fringe benefits do you get: shower, stove, jacuzzi, got a pool in there? How's the stereo, hydraulic seats? Wouldn't it be nice to be a computer whiz when they're putting your order in — just get in there and tap in a few extras."

Bunny throws a few barbs at the Canadian forces. "Look-ing tough but running scared." A soldier breaks over the con-versation: "We're a peacekeeping nation, not a warmaking nation." Manny says "You carry guns, they're for killing people aren't they?"

I tell Manny how, at Wookey Hole, Alexander Pope had stolen a lot of the stalactites. He brought in a troop of muske-teers to shoot them down. Pope used the pendant and curtain for his Grotto in Twickenham. The Nazis dropped a bomb on the Grotto so all we have left are the gaps in Wookey. While we were digging, academics studied the gaps. Trying to recreate the Grotto from what was absent.

Manny said he'd been stationed in Germany before he got married. "It's a fine country. They treat you fine." But his wife got sick of him gone. He got out, started trucking.

"Norma left saying I was never home and I didn't bring enough in. That's what she said. But it wasn't true. The religion took her. I gave her eight hundred a week for expenses and food for two, kept two-fifty for my needs on the road. I got me a sleeper so it's pretty cheap. But that couldn't do her. Said she was lonely. Sure I took her on the road. Used to drive her out to her folks. I'd go an hour off the road for that. Pick her up on the way back. That was when I was Independent. I'd come home there'd be no money and her closet full of clothes. Price tags still on half of it. She thought bar codes were evil. You could make 666 out of the stripes. Sixty thousand for the house. Stove, fridge and all the curtains."

I look at the hands around Suzie. They are thin hands with a ring.

"Often wanted to go again. Not Germany. Go to Kuwait, that way. Lots of jobs trucking."

The windshield catches a few pecks of rain and they shiver over to the margins.

"You see much of her?" I point to the photo. Manny shakes his head.

"All our friends turned out to be Norma's friends. So I don't see Suzie. I used to, I mean I can be with her twice a month. But I don't have a house. The first little while was all right, but then she grew away. Kept wanting to go back to Mom. She was only three. Forgetting who I was. Bill, he works for Big Wheel, he was telling me if he'd put in the work on the first marriage he's putting into the second, he'd still be with it."

Zuza married Wenxiong so he could stay in Canada. It was a political move. They went to China for a year. Zuza taught ESL and Wenxiong worked at the university. Wenxiong's parents asking when were they returning to Canada. No-one expected them to stay more than a few weeks. Zuza wrote saying tourists are tolerated, but a Westerner married to a Chinese is frowned upon. It takes a long time to make friends. In fact, she hadn't made any. "No-one invites me without asking Wenxiong too. And they ask him first."

There's nothing sadder than feeling lonely and never being alone. "I hate to generalize," she wrote, "but I find it ridiculous that Chinese live so close and refuse to touch each other."

Manny says "If I had my time, you know what I wish I'd known? Two things." He points a V at the window wipers. "I wish I'd been more sure of things. You know what I'm saying? Confidence. The other thing — the power of compound interest. It's all you hear now. But twenty years ago, nothing."

The way he looks at me makes it clear I can add a regret. The truck behind us swerves from side to side.

"You can't even run together. Big Wheel doesn't like it. Figure we stop for coffee and gab too long. We're not supposed to pick up people, but that's where I call it. You got a sign and you got no gun."

The army convoy signals. Slowly they pull off into a campground. Manny has to gear down quickly. I once had a shoulder dislocated, and the way the doctor guided the bone into the socket describes the skill Manny used to manoeuvre through thirteen gears. The wire fence has a sign that mentions National Defense.

"War games. They're going to play Cowboys and Indians."

Bunny Wheeler passes, honking.

"She always had a touch of religion, but then with Suzie she went all the way. I said Norma I don't want you raising her like that. But I was gone. She turned right around. Going to bible study. Suzie'd show me the hymn book, with Joseph and the baby Lord Jesus. She loved the babies. Maybe it was Jesus blessing a baby."

Jesus visited Wookey Hole. Manny doesn't believe it. I mention how Jesus' great uncle Joseph was a tin merchant. He took Jesus with him to Cornwall. They stayed in Glastonbury and no doubt went down to Wookey Hole. Some say it was Jesus who showed his uncle how to extract tin, how to separate it from wolfram. Jesus was twenty-seven. My age. Digging the same soil.

"She got everything different except the smoking. You know they don't know what a habit it is. Norma had this little red machine about yay long."

Manny pokes his forefingers out from the wheel.

"Like one of those machines they roll over your credit card. Neat little rig. I used to roll them for her, they're fun doing. You get the tobacco and a box of tubes and you line up the one and push the tobacco through. And chung out it pops. One time the thing broke. And you know she can't smoke the bought kind. They pack them too tight. Can't get a draw through, she'd say. I mean her breath's gone. She went crazy until I fixed the spring. I bought a new one for a back-up."

I tell him how I walked to Bethlehem from Jerusalem. Artillery shells pounding the horizon. The first building in Bethlehem, just passed Rachel's Tomb, is the Bethlehem Cigarette and Tobacco Company.

We pass through some small towns. One is geared up for selling worms and hubcaps. Little wooden signs the size of mailboxes with bleached words and an arrow pointing to a backyard or a shed decorated with hubcaps.

"Later on it's berries and corn," Manny says.

Then an overpass: BRIDGE FREEZES BEFORE ROAD.

"You get signs like that all over," Manny says. "Signs that are out of season. You feel like gearing down anyway. Like Slippery When Wet. On a dry day your foot goes on the brake."

A couple near the bridge with their thumbs out. No sign.

"I was heading back west after a job. Empty trailer. I picked up every hitchhiker I came on. Put them in the back. I must have had thirty on board, one time. Had a list of where they wanted to go. You can't see a thing in the trailer. And they'd talk. Couldn't see a hand. Every time I stopped they'd all peer out. Trying to get their bearings. Check their watches and look at maps, betting on where they were. The next guy getting in would think I had a trap. I can still see the look. But they'd jump in. A couple of girls didn't, so I had them in the sleeper. See, that curtain pulls across."

I look in back. He has a thermos on a blanket. There's a garage calendar with a woman holding a wrench.

"Never any trouble. And sometimes you get a piece." He winks. "I got a lot of postcards. There's some on your shade."

They are tucked in with an elastic band. Pictures of New Mexico, P.E.I., Alberta.

"You can take down the address." It is care of Big Wheel.

"One of Norma's friends at Bible study had a garden. Made her fed up with all the junk I had in back, the engines and the come-along, the wood piled up — I sell wood. So I bought her a few flowers and that was good for nine yards. I pass this nursery in Fredericton and I picked up a few things they figured she could handle. And she had a lot of interest in that. She'd rush in with something that had blown off.

'Smell it' she'd say and I would but all I could smell was the cigarette off her hands."

Those hands around Suzie.

"She's from the bible belt. People moved up in the seventies. They got that KKK feel down in Tennessee. You pull up for diesel and they come out at you with this smile on like they're going to drill you if you put your foot wrong. Big grin saying, You want a cup of coffee? Holding a plastic mug. Checking out the rig like you got a hundred coloreds in there. Creepy."

We pass some gravel pits. Bulldozers carving into the hill. "I got my own views on that stuff you're into," Manny says. "Like you say, older stuff is further down. Well what about this. The trees get leaves right? From the sun. Sun makes the leaves. That energy and mass stuff. Einstein. You follow me? So the leaves fall off and soil gets deeper. But now all the time the earth is getting heavier. All this soil. Over the years, hundreds of years. Earth gets heavier and the distance —" he pauses to think, "the distance from the sun goes greater. Big planets are out further. So the earth cools off. That's what I figure. We're heading for a big one. Big ice age."

The road follows the shoreline of a lake. The water makes me sleepy. We're bogged in a bit of traffic and Manny puts the tape on again.

The lake is large. It could be the sea. Down by the bridge where there's shelter. Mrs Scanlon's saltbox. The site in her backyard. The dig is going well. Someone has found a chert knife. I'm working an area near Mrs Scanlon's compost. She's the only person in the cove with a compost. Helps her potatoes. She tells me to tear my teabags. Won't rot otherwise. My partner a thin woman, smoking. It's Manny's wife, but she speaks Slovak. We measure the depth of the excavation. She takes a black and white picture. She carries a cloth bag. The bag holds a Bible and the cigarette maker. We're scraping away with our trowels and we find a hand. A small, fresh hand. As if we'd just buried it. We work down the arm to the shoulder. We use our fingers because the trowels could do damage. The soil crumbles like cake. The head emerges. The eyes are closed and the mouth is set firm. It's Suzie with the fish. Norma lifts the child, pulls her out like a worm, raises her in the air. "*Dieťa je preč,*" she says, shaking her head.

I hold Norma, to comfort her, and when I turn to look at her she's Zuza. I feel the cry tremble through her back.

The trees are darker, the road bluer. I have an erection. Manny has flicked on the lights. We've left the lake.

"You were gone awhile," he says.

"I didn't get much sleep."

Manny looks set to gear down.

"I got to fill up at this Irving. You might get a ride through."

The lights of Moncton are flickering on. The Lutes Mountain Irving is cleaning up after the supper run. Manny drives in behind to the diesel pumps. I thank him and he wishes me luck.

Quick as that we part. I go inside and sit at a booth. It's rapidly getting dark. I order fish and chips and a coffee. The batter thin and fresh.

I leave a fair tip. When you sleep cheap you can eat well. In the Men's I wash my face and hands. I twist up the nozzle of the hand dryer, close my eyes. I brush my teeth. In the mirror I still look young.

At the self-serve pumps I pass a man I'd known in university. His car is pointing east and I think about asking. He's in a tie and jacket. But he doesn't recognize me and I think, he hasn't changed in ten years. And I laugh because I haven't either.

I cross the highway and find a dirt road. It leads to a house with shake siding. I go back to a clear patch in the trees. I test the ground with my feet. I find a piece of cardboard and put that down. Then I unroll my sleeping bag. Lutes Mountain Irving is shining bright straight across from me. The cars race by like rockets.

I lie here looking at the stars creeping out. In the morning I'll see blueberries creeping out of the green. At Wookey Hole a couple of us took a trip north. We passed Rugby Clock, which is a field filled with scientific instruments. It keeps precise time for the world. It's the place of Zero Hour. This green field with small towers of mechanical objects. There were no scientists or cows even. Just the still field, keeping a record of time passing.

Remember how Zuza had said Chinese cover their mouths when they pick their teeth. We were listening to orbu music, eating litchi fruit and drinking Hungarian sherry.

I told her how at Wookey I watched a stalagmite join a stalactite. They grow about an inch every thousand years. The two were separated by a hair. Then, as if a spark of life ignited, a tiny crystal filament leapt up and the teeth became a bar.

The kids are hanging out on the bridge in Port au Choix. Their names spray-painted on the guard rail. A lot of O'Keefes. Instead of their whole names, they just put Billy O'K and Jimmy O'K and Jason O'K. As if that is enough.

Poorest Tourist

■ ■ ■

The oasis: two eucalyptus and an orange tree Magdi's uncle had planted thirty years before. He was a dowser. Dug a hole and hit a seam of water the size of your arm. Enough to satisfy his camels.

Magdi shoves the well cover aside. Hauls up ten meters of rope. Water's gone down, he says, indicating the indentation of the land. We are in the Saqqarat depression. Around us stand huge calcium deposits carved like apple cores. We are roughly a hundred miles west of the Nile. Magdi gives us twenty minutes for pictures.

Mark says "It's just like Australia. I can't believe how much it's like Australia."

Mark keeps seeing acacias, tea trees. He says "Look, there's an acacia." But we're in trains or buses, and by the time I have looked, the acacia is gone.

Now Matthias Rehm says "Look, an acacia," pointing behind me. And when I turn there's only the White Desert and the apple cores. "Oh, it's gone," he says. Then he ducks behind one of the apples to urinate.

The Peugeot sinks down and the horizon edges upward. The sky is a camera flash. And you get used to looking down the barrel of your nose at the blur of sand. The horizon greets us every ten minutes.

Magdi stops the car by a pile of bricks scattered on the

road. "Bricks from a truck on its way to Farafra." We help him toss them over the edge of sand. We think this is a safety measure, that Magdi is concerned other vehicles may not see the bricks. But then he leaves one as a marker on top of a dune. The dune has its lip lying over most of the road. Magdi takes a long look at a distant hill, his hand shading his eyes. Then he jumps back in the car. Bricks are valuable. He'll pick them up on his way back.

The seats are soaked. Our pants and shirts are wet, anything in the shade. The corduroy cover on the steering wheel is dry at the top and wet at the bottom. Matthias and Mark are smoking at the windows. I ride on the hump. Mark is in front. Magdi maneuvers around the dune drift. He is weak from Ramadan.

We slow down near the hill. A plain mound rising out of the middle of the White Desert. Magdi puts one hand on his hip and with the other makes a grand gesture towards the mound. "This is the tomb of René," he declares.

The mastaba is capped with concrete. 1937-1986 has been fingered roughly into the cement.

"Who is René?"

Magdi cocks his head. "Everyone wants to see René." He looks away, rolls his eyes. He climbs back in the car.

On the outskirts of Farafra Magdi stops. "You must get out here." Ahead there is a checkpoint, and Magdi cannot bring us in. "You must walk through. Then I will meet you."

Matthias protests. "At least bring us closer."

"This is fifty meters."

The smudge on the horizon is a good two kilometers away. Magdi relents. "If I am caught I will lose my car."

He crawls in second gear. He stops after one kilometer. "This is far as I go. Fifty meters is not a big walk."

"But it's not fifty meters."

He won't budge. "You must also take your bags."

We watch him fly through the checkpoint. As we approach we see more desert beyond the gate.

The guard requests assistance. We pool together 5000 lira.

"He says he has a headache."

"He wants drugs."

Mark checks his bag. He counts out six painkillers.

In Farafra we eat rice and zucchini in a clay-walled café that is thick with flies. There are blinds on the windows. Mark listens to Keith Jarret's Köln Concert on his walkman. A Belgian, who has been in Farafra for eight months, watercoloring the same desert landscape a thousand times over, tells us René was a famous tour guide. He wanted to be buried in the Libyan Desert. The Belgian chuckles. "René is now his own landmark."

A Sudanese cook in a floppy white hat pours the çay and then kneels on a green mat. Matthias adjusts his red-framed glasses. He tells the Belgian how we drove from Aswan to Abu Simbel and back. "All in one morning. We spent thirty minutes at the site. It was like driving from Stuttgart to Paris just to see the Louvre for half an hour."

What we have done in Egypt sounds vaguely impressive. Mark says all that he has done has been done to him.

In Singapore, Matthias says, when they know you are German the first thing they say is Sieg Heil.

"And what can you do?" He used to try to explain "Oh no, you mustn't do that, that's not good." And they would look at him strange. In the Far East, he says, they sell *Mein Kampf* in the shops. Because of the war. They were British colonies, French, Danish. They thought things had to be this way. Fatalism. Then suddenly they see a man defeating their enemies. Hitler arms them and eventually they are independent. He is a hero. To be revered.

"And you are German traveling in their country and you tell them, No, *Mein Kampf* is not a good book and you must not Heil Hitler me. No, they think you are crazy or a wanker. So now when they do it and they do it often I just smile and say Right mate, finish my beer and move on."

Magdi invites us to see his uncle's workshop. The shop is tiny and ill-lit. The uncle, an old man now, is moulding clay vessels on a footpowered wheel. The clay jiggles in his hands, like water, as he sculpts. He lifts it high into the air, holding it against gravity's pull until it is stiff enough to hold its own.

The uncle is lit only by light from the door. His foot kicks the wheel at a constant speed. Matthias hauls out his camera gear. Mark does the same. Suddenly the workshop is bright with camera lightning. They move in for close-ups, squint through their lenses, adjust the focus. They kneel, stand far back, and make sure they have captured every conceivable angle. They talk to each other from behind their cameras, hardly noticing Magdi's edginess.

Afterwards they place some money on the uncle's workbench. He nods without showing any expression, continuing to raise the clay into form.

We wander down to a spring to bathe. The water is as warm as blood. Beyond the eucalyptus and behind a low wall stand several fruit trees. I take out my sketch pad. The long limbs poke holes through the eucalyptus, allowing light through their net. As I fill in some detail I notice a boy sitting in the crotch of one of the trees. He is tearing fruit from the branches. He spies me spying him and quickly descends. He walks along the low wall I am on, kneels, looks over my shoulder at the picture. He offers a nectarine. I bite into it. It is juicy, very ripe.

Queiss.

Good.

I tear out the page. He takes it, scans the area above, nods. He rolls the paper into a funnel then leaps down to run along the path out of sight. From behind I hear Magdi calling: "Canada Dry," he cries. "Canada Dry, we are leaving."

The edge of land and light blur as the Peugeot putters on with Magdi and Matthias in the front, Mark and me in the back. A huge bird lifts off the road ahead and barely works its progress as we pass under. The car bumps over roadkill. Magdi laughs over his shoulder. He swerves the Peugeot around dunes, making the plastic fruit on the rear view mirror lurch. Then he laughs, wipes his eyes.

"You are hysterical to watch," Mark says.

We stop again. Magdi points out some bleached branches.

"For fire," he says proudly, as if he has made or caught the wood himself. He takes a red canister from the boot and refills the gas tank.

"We are eating and fire we need to boil rice and tea."

The trees are far from the road and the sand sucks at our feet. The branches are easy to pull up. There do not seem to be roots. Magdi lashes the branches to the roof. Gunther takes a photo of us picking wood.

We are on the edge. On the edge of light and dust that are fusing into the same color. Ahead, a dark shape appears and your eyes naturally tend to hover on it. The dot grows edges and form and soon enough it is a truck. Magdi shifts down as a huge white tent folds out of the sand. Arabs move about slowly, preparing blankets, carefully handling wooden bowls that are heavy with steam.

"All I wanted," says Matthias, stretching his back, "was

two weeks on the beach at Alexandria. And here I am in the middle of a goddamn desert with a bunch of crazy people." He reaches for his camera, but Magdi puts a hand on the strap. "No pictures." He jogs over to a flap in the tent. Mark kneels in the hot sand. "Life is your film," he says, pouring sand from his hand in meditation. He has two degrees, one in Law, one in the Fine Arts. He measures the sand, tries to make a calculation from his sample. A math that will explain this landscape.

Magdi reappears, leads us over to the blankets. A tall Arab checks his wrist and looks at the thin wide sun. Magdi talks to him, tosses his head our way and they both laugh soberly. "Come," the tall Arab says, lifting his long dark arm and pulling the air to him.

We follow what Magdi does. Folding our legs on the blanket. Matthias says he is always surprised at how hard sand is. The wooden bowls we surround contain boiled potatoes, lamb mutton and another has diced tomatoes. The Arab walks a few paces toward the sun and checks his wrist again. He is tall, isolated from everything. But when Mark passes him he shrinks in size. Mark is no more than five foot ten.

Other men mill about. There are only men, repairing the road and now waiting for the fast to break. Waiting for the sun.

Magdi trots over to the Peugeot. He unties the branches, towering them over his head like a nest, and walks ungainly back. A black smoke puffs from the head of the tent.

The men sit down with us and one, Hamet, who knows a little German and some English, translates. They want to know of Israel, of what is happening there. "Hitler," he says, "was not such a bad man."

The cook appears with pita bread and the men greet him lovingly, touching his shoulder gracefully, and he looks glad to be their cook. Someone asks the Arab with the watch if it is time and he says it is. Twenty to seven.

"So you have been to Cairo?" Hamet asks.

"That's where we met."

They laugh and it's plain to see they laugh a lot.

"Which do you prefer: Cairo," and Hamet stretches his arms wide to take in the land about him, "or the Saqqarat?"

We look at each other. Mark answers "The Saqqarat," and they grin approvingly.

"You like the pyramids though?"

We shrug and say the pyramids are fine. They know then that we do not want to say that the Egyptians in Cairo and Giza and Luxor and Aswan, the Egyptians along the Nile's tourist strip, have transformed into money changers, alabaster sellers and camel-ride hawkers.

A jug of water is passed around and we hesitate. Again the men laugh. "From deep well in Farafra," Hamet says.

We eat while the sun has one last look around its borders. The desert reaches out on all sides with no disturbance. Every place that becomes familiar is where the heart longs to return. And here there is a slow revolving pace that does not care for its own completion. The men eat their food, oblivious to the road that needs repair. It will wait and be finished when it forgets its purpose.

Hamet turns to me. "You like the çay?"

"It's the best I have had since Turkey," I tell him.

We eat with these twenty men beside their paving truck, the hard red blankets and the flapping tent. The silent Peugeot and the dark brown faces. The men do not care where we are from. They share with respect, which is without doubt.

After the tea we rise and thank them. They stand by the edge of new pavement and watch us go. Their paving truck and tent recede into the vast darkening day. We head for nothing in particular. The seats are stiff. Magdi guides the Peugeot along the narrow strip of asphalt. The land and sky are smooth and black from neglect. The night is not cold, and very silent for such a large thing. We have been used to the rough and now, on this band of paved road, it feels as if we are flying.

The Charity Sisters

■ ■ ■

Bob Hillier's sister, Margaret, had started up a thrift shop. Four years the elder, Margaret Hillier had turned to religion, had become involved in the Charity Sisters, a faction of the Pentecostal faith. She needed someone to take the cash in the afternoons. Bob would do it.

Bob Hillier had studied social work in university. He had wanted to work with the police on crime, but instead of being confronted with difficult casework, identifying causes of death, pinning killers, he had to cope with grieving survivors of suicide, family beatings and child abuse.

He quit. He decided to study for the Law School Admission Test. He failed. He applied for work with the Canadian Security Intelligence Service. Again, he pictured tracking suspects through foreign destinations, an umbrella with a laser beam, an edible button that poisoned him.

Upon arrival at the Academy he was lectured on perseverance. The waiting game. Hours, days, sitting patiently. A network of teams on shiftwork, the surveillance of extreme political parties, the headquarters of native bands. Labor meetings. The antics of executives in supermarket chains. Wait and be ready for commands. The office had walls two feet thick.

The Charity Sisters was located on the corner of New Gower and Waldegrave. The Radisson Hotel across the street, an Ultramar gas station to the left. Public housing on the right. Margaret lived in the apartment above. She had a son, Luke, from a man she met in France six years ago. That was when Margaret had exhausted her search for earthly satisfaction, a reason for incarnation. Francois Rosinante had sent a photo and one letter when Luke was born. In raw English he described the tears in his heart — rips or sadness — and his commitment to supplying the new McDonald's in Marseilles with quality beef patties.

Bob remembers his wild sister. Margaret used to sneak men into her bedroom. He would hear the rubbing against the wall. She would show her boyfriends how to break into the house. The Hilliers owned porcelain from Occupied Japan, brass plates, artifacts from the sea. Margaret showed the men basement windows left unlatched, the coal scuttle entrance, the extra room with Mother-in-Law door above the kitchen. She planned robberies when her parents were gone to parties.

The Charity Sisters was supplied with clothing from a number of church outlets. The bags sorted. The clothing too worn for resale torn into strips and sold as rags to the Ultramar across the street. Mostly women's clothes — the men's went to the penitentiary. The sorting and tearing done in a room in back by a mentally challenged student from the HUB. The Charity Sisters had received funding to hire Todd for three afternoons each week. Todd worked the washer, dryer and ironing board. A rag cutter pointed its chrome wings to the four corners. A window looked out on a parking lot, a maple and a narrow view of the harbor and the Atlantic.

Bob liked the locale. He could watch the hotel across the street, which housed the rich visitors to his city. He spied on the gas station for hold-ups, taxi deliveries, unusual pick-ups. The public housing came through the wall. Conversations. All sorts strolled into the Charity Sisters store to either drop off or pick through suits, shirts, pants, curtains, children's clothes.

One day it was a young couple. They looked astonished. That would be the tenderest word to describe their faces, Bob thought. For they were poor people who had not yet discovered thrift stores. Their faces showed an amazement at the variety and quality of goods he could offer them.

"This coat would fit you nice," the man said. He had to shout, for the woman had squirreled away into a separate corner.

"No, Mel, I don't like blue."

Mel held it up a while longer. It was a nice coat. Mel had taste. But it was blue.

The woman was breathing hard into a box of purses and leather goods. Belts, sandals.

Mel sifted through the barrel of men's shoes. He pulled up a long cowboy boot. "This is all right."

He searched for the partner. It was there. Bob had put them out yesterday. They were an excellent pair of boots. A man from the hotel had looked both ways, crossed on the hand, running, placed them on the counter and said, "These you can have." A golden cornflake color, with leather soles and a layered leather heel. Taps. Tooled. A size too small for Bob. And Todd didn't like them.

Mel found the left foot and paired them up to his shoes. "Lana, these are some boots."

Mel turned to Bob, hoisting up the boots. "How much?"

There was a list of prices in front of Mel. Bob said "Two fifty."

"Two fifty. Man, that's all right. I can go for that." He turned to Lana. "Two fifty, Lana."

"Try them on, Mel. You got to try them on."

"No, I can see they fit."

Mel put them up to his shoes again. "These," he said

emphatically, "are beautiful."

He told Lana that he was just going down to the bank to get some money. "You stay here and I'll be back." He turned to Bob. "I can donate these shoes?" He held up his foot. Bob noted the three blue stars in the web of his thumb. "You don't buy things, do you?"

Bob said he wasn't in a position to buy anything.

"No, I'll donate these shoes."

"You don't want to do that, Mel. The shoes are good. Keep the shoes."

"I got the boots now, Lana."

"But you don't have to give up the shoes."

"I'll be wearing the boots."

"But you can carry the shoes."

"I don't want to be walking around with a bag of shoes under my arm."

"But, Mel."

He inched his way out the door. "I'm just going down to the bank to get twenty dollars. I'll play some Instant Pick and then be back, okay? And I'm giving him the shoes."

Lana watched his back. Then she went for the coats hanging. Her breath loud, almost snoring. She turned to the pants. She paused on one pair.

"You can try them on."

Bob showed her where. She had a patch of chafed skin under her nose and her hair was greasy in the roots. "Thank-you," she said.

Lana had been in about a minute when one of the Ultramar mechanics came over.

"Ragtime."

Bob said he'd check in back. Todd was stretching his arms against the wings of the rag cutter. For a second he looked like a melting Icarus. Todd nodded to a fresh bag.

When Bob came out with the rags, the mechanic was trying on Mel's boots.

"These are all right," he said, checking the mirror. He reached into his coveralls. "Two fifty?"

"Yes," Bob said. "Two fifty."

"Can you put them in a bag?"

Lana waited for Mel. She said "You just wait, mister" for an hour, but no Mel. She sat on a box of children's clothes and breathed while customers circulated. She was hard to see, but you heard the breathing. You knew someone was hiding under the tails of shirts up ahead. Then you saw the knees in blue tights sticking out, the brown shoes. But Mel didn't come back.

At five thirty Bob said, "I lock up now." But Lana didn't budge. When the bus came Todd put on his coat and said so long. Bob said to Lana "You'll have to go," but just the wheeze.

"Come on now. Mel's not coming back."

"But he said he would."

"He's probably forgotten where you are."

She sat on that while Bob did the cash. Then she said "I can't believe you sold his boots."

"Did he come back?"

"He went to get the money."

She got off the box. Bob wrapped a rubber band on the money. Left the cash drawer open. He felt bad about the boots. He could have said to the mechanic, "Sorry, but there's a guy who's just gone to get the money." But it was one of those moments when you have to say something quickly to stop a process, to halt the future. And at that moment Bob had felt lethargic.

"Now you have to go," he said to Lana.

"I got nowhere to go."

Bob said, "Where'd you come from?"

"Mel's," she said.

"Well, go to Mel's."

"But he's gone."

"He's probably waiting for you."

"He's not waiting."

"Why don't you call him."

Bob touched the phone. But she shook her head. "Got no phone."

"Well where do you live. Or where's Mel's."

Lana lifted the toes of her shoes.

"The truck is Mel's."

A truck camper. Mel had been parked off Merrymeeting Road. In Gilbert's Court.

"He's got a woodstove in there," she said. "It's real cosy. He got a TV and a crib board. Stars on the roof."

Bob's sister came down the stairs. "Hello," she said.

"Margaret, this is Lana."

"Are we closed?"

Bob explained the situation.

"Well, Lana, why don't you come up."

Luke was having beans on toast in front of the TV. Flicking Francois Rosinante's gold hair out of his eyes.

"Luke, this is Lana."

"Hi. Hi Bob."

They discussed what to do. Lana's family down in Goose Bay. She described a town in Labrador just on the Quebec border. The mine shut down. The company took out everything. Folded up prefab homes, the lot. She was back there last summer, for a visit. She drove along streets she used to play on as a kid. Just rectangles of foundations. Here and there a fire hydrant.

She saw a little girl in a blue dress stroking a set of wind chimes in a tree. This used to be their doorbell, the girl said.

"That's all that's left," Lana said. Here, she doesn't know anyone besides Mel.

"He just drove into Goose one day. Said he always wanted to get in one of those jets. He parked at the fence and watched them take off. Barbecued pork chops right by the fence."

Bob drove her up to Merrymeeting. They checked Gilbert Court. No truck camper. Lana pointed out an oil patch on the pavement. "The pan leaks."

Margaret called the Carolyn Center. They had a bed. "You could stay there," she said.

Mel had intended on coming back, getting the boots and Lana. He had withdrawn twenty dollars. He'd chosen four Instant Pick. The best he had was two oranges. Then he realized he could give up the boots. If he didn't return he could get in the truck and drive off. It was nice for March. The trees had little buds that looked like umbrellas half open. He walked briskly to the gas station. Black-capped chickadees sang from a wire. He had parked across from the store, in back of the Ultramar. He jammed the shifter into drive. He watched a mechanic at the air hose trying on a pair of cowboy boots. Another man in the same green overalls was drinking from a styrofoam cup, yelling "Whoa, Daddy! Lasso me a chickeroo."

Mel held the steering wheel firmly. He thought that most people are living their lives, hoping that when they die they won't live on. If they had life after death they'd be disappointed, almost shamed by the way they had been living. The guy in the used clothing store was like that. Had nothing in him suggesting anything bigger. At least Lana had a hold on something. She would tell him about the abyss. How she saw all these people falling into a huge hole, smiling, all of them unaware. Just falling into a pit, millions of people. He kept a *National Geographic* copy of El Greco's *Fellipe II's Dream* which has a blind maw feeding on humans, their backs turned to it, like how you are supposed to catch caplin with a dip net. Four rough white teeth and nostrils flaming with some inner light. But what did that mean? What are you supposed to do?

A month later, during Tenebrae, Mel meets Margaret Hillier at the Charity Sisters' foodbank. He invites her for a cup of tea in his truck camper. He lights the propane, draws water from a plastic barrel. He drains a tin of Vienna sausages. She remarks on the woodstove. He tells her he is excited by her zest, her spirit. He says he likes to live too close to what is real. As they talk, the light diminishes and stars appear on his ceiling.

Hands

■ ■ ■

He'd talked with a wide-eyed frantic woman and a guard who was behind the tall wrought-iron fence of Buckingham Palace. It was the first time he'd spoken more than a full sentence in over three days. He strolled past Chelsea stadium and staggered up Earl's Court. He drank tea in a chip shop. He urinated in Fleet Street. He walked over Tower bridge, passed the London Dungeon, noticed the TO LET signs, followed cobbled roads until they turned into dirt. By the time he took the path to the hostel his watch said 3 a.m. Perhaps it was open.

Near the entrance were the silhouettes of several young men standing alert. They looked like they were planning to break in to one of the adjacent houses. Then Marshall saw a balding man at the hostel gate and decided they were all on guard to stop latecomers sneaking in. He walked past them, along the path which wound up and around. A few more stood in the bush. A streetlamp turned the leaves yellow. Soon he heard steps behind him. Carefully, he took out his pocketknife and slipped it into the palm of his glove. The brass casing pressed into his flesh. The man passed and they looked at each other.

When the path ended, on Kensington again, Marshall saw the man leaning on a rail and smiled at him. The man immediately approached Marshall, offered his hand and called himself

Muhammad, his car was just back there, and would Marshall like to go home with him for a drink. Marshall shook hands with his gloves on, the knife inside between their palms. "I'm very tired," he said. "I've been up since yesterday morning and it's London."

Muhammad laughed and said no problem, nothing to worry, and they compromised on a walk back to his car. Muhammad was Egyptian and Marshall told him that he intended to go to Egypt, that he was waiting for a flight to Athens this coming Wednesday. That he would travel through Turkey and Israel before entering the Sinai.

They passed the shadows outside the hostel gate and one of the men nodded towards Muhammad who closed his eyes and lifted his chin. Marshall asked him why were they there. He was ready to believe that they were waiting for the hostel to open. Travelers with no luggage. But Muhammad said they were 'cruising'.

There was a Mercedes-Benz in the parking lot and Marshall offered his hand with the knife as a goodbye. "No, no," Muhammad said. "That doesn't stop us two from talking. If you are going to Egypt you must get used to hospitality."

He had a flat, he said, and Marshall had until seven to kill, why not have a cup of coffee? a talk?

"It's cold. You have four hours. You can rest in the car at least."

Marshall agreed to sit in the car. Muhammad found some disco new-wave Indian music on the radio. The knife lay wet, the spine of the blade warm, inside the glove.

"Let me take you for a spin. Not to my place. Just around the block. I have someone to meet."

The street names whizzed past, and in the dark it was difficult to catch them. The car had British steering and Marshall was not used to sitting on the left with the wheel on the right. He found his foot pressed to the floor where the brake pedal should be.

With each successive gear Muhammad turned the music up a notch. The speed felt good in the car. The roads were damp and the tires had good traction. It felt crazy sitting in the driver's seat with no wheel. It was like being in the front of a train, the car set on rails destined to follow a certain route.

They were in an unknown corner of London. Muhammad braked and swerved across the road to the curb where a tall black man stood. Muhammad rolled the window down and leaned an elbow out. The man bent over and handed Muhammad a full zippered pouch. They exchanged a few words in Arabic. Muhammad reached out and held the man's arm. Marshall could see the man's head, cropped afro. Muhammad slapped the arm and rolled the window up.

"Who was that?"

"A friend I work with."

They motored on to another man who was waiting, a little bored, near a letterbox. Again they spoke in Arabic. This time the man got in the back seat behind Muhammad. "Faroukh, this is my friend Marshall." He geared down as a car approached, winking its headlights. Muhammad leaned out and clasped hands with the driver. They spoke softly. Faroukh slouched across the back seat, his knees pressing into Marshall's seat.

Muhammad dropped Faroukh off near a post office. "I live just here if you would like to see the place," he said, turning onto an even smaller street.

"I'd prefer just to go back."

"You can kip at my place. I have two beds. No problem. Or you can rest until seven. There is no point in going back until seven."

He backed into a parking space. Turned off the music.

"Come. You can rest here."

As they took the grated steps to the third landing, Marshall felt his waist for the traveler's checks. The car had been hot and now the sweat cooled on his back.

Muhammad showed him into the kitchen. Marshall sat at the table in his coat and gloves. He felt foolish wearing the gloves, but he didn't want to lose the knife. He knew it would take less than three seconds to pull the glove off and open the blade. So he sat there with his coat on, his gloved hands on his lap.

Muhammad filled an aluminum pot and put it on the stove. He selected dance music on the radio. "I like this music," he said, leaning from side to side. He twisted his head like a tired fish on a hook.

The kitchen was lit by a fluorescent coil in the ceiling. The apartment was new, the walls very white. There were no mouldings or baseboards. There was a calendar on the cupboard door. January featured three nude men from the knees up. One man cupped the soft genitalia of another while the third coddled up behind, placing his hands on the man's thighs. All three caught the eye of the viewer.

"Would you like a —" Muhammad pursed his fingers to his mouth, inhaled, then, holding his breath, offered the fingers to Marshall.

"No. Thanks."

When the water boiled Muhammad made instant coffee. "I usually make coffee in the microwave. But there was lightning and the microwave blew up."

Marshall found this hard to believe.

"Really. It sort of fizzled the back. The whole building had things go out. I never use it really. Only to boil water. You have to watch because if you heat something and take it out it is still getting hotter. It heats from the inside out. You can drink something warm which begins to boil in your throat."

Marshall took off a glove to hold the cup. He undid the zipper on his raincoat.

Muhammad smoked two joints filled with hash using the screw method. He kept his stash in a Marmite jar in the cupboard behind the calendar. He lit them on the element he'd used to boil water.

"So what do you know of Egypt?"

"I know the Nile is there. The pyramids. I want to go to Mount Sinai."

"Why Mount Sinai?"

Marshall rubbed the sharp hair on his chin. "My brother used to call it Mount Cyanide. The poison? He used to call Alsatian dogs 'Salvation' dogs. It sounds like a place you should see for yourself."

"You have seen German Shepherds?"

Alsatians.

Muhammad had mellowed. He grooved to the radio. He wiped spilt coffee off the counter. Marshall felt as if his name weren't Muhammad at all, but Randy. Suddenly he stopped wavering. "Do you know anyone in Egypt?"

"No."

"Do you want to know someone?"

"You have family?"

"I have friends. My family — maybe not."

"Where do they live?"

"In Cairo. You are going to Cairo. If you want to see the pyramids you have to go to Cairo."

"Have you seen the pyramids?"

"Have you seen Niagara Falls? No, I have seen them. They are stones. This high."

Muhammad lifted his arm out straight from his shoulder. Marshall couldn't tell if he meant the pyramids were puny or that they were made of stones this high.

"Do you want to see magic?"

"Sure."

Muhammad pulled out a drawer and rummaged through what looked like a stack of chopsticks. He took out two blue sponges.

He turned the radio down a notch but he still had to shout over it. "I will put one blue in my hand like so and I give you the other. Please —"

He beckoned for the hand with the glove on. Marshall peeled it off, shaking the knife down into a finger.

"And I give you this one. Now concentrate on the blue in your hand. It is melting. Slowly it is getting smaller. You cannot feel it, can you?"

Marshall thought he felt the sponge, but he couldn't tell for sure. He figured Muhammad had both sponges. But it still felt as if one was in his hand. Marshall had seen the sponge go in. Felt the coarseness of the snipped bubbles. Muhammad held his hand tightly beside Marshall's.

"Perhaps we should see what is in my hand."

Muhammad released his fingers and his palm was empty. "Then you must have my blue. Open!"

Marshall opened his fingers and two blue sponges popped out. Muhammad grinned, collected the sponges, and tossed them back into the drawer.

"Would you like to watch telly?"

There was no set to be seen.

"It is in the other room. Come."

The other room was the bedroom. There were two single beds separated by a digital clock radio on a nightstand. A closet was built into the wall. The TV sat on top of a chest of drawers. A lamp stood on the TV and cast an X-shaped glow over the wall.

Muhammad straddled the closest bed and Marshall took the other.

"Please, come. Sit up here." Muhammad patted the bedspread.

"I'm fine here, really."

The gloves were on the kitchen table.

An American college football game was into the third quarter. Washington State led by three and they were on their own thirty. Marshall realized it would be late afternoon on the Pacific coast. That they were watching the same sun he'd seen yesterday. He was hopelessly tired.

"Why don't you sleep? Let me undress you."

"No, really. I'm fine. I'd like to watch."

They stared at the game for fifteen minutes, each trying to show an interest. At the end of the quarter Muhammad said "It is about as sensible as cricket." He turned to Marshall, rubbing his groin. "Can you help me with this? I'm so hard."

He reached for Marshall's hand, trying to press it to his jeans.

Marshall rose. "I have to go now."

"What is wrong? If two people want to come and they can help each other . . ."

"I want to go."

"Oh please. Sit down. I don't mean to spoil your time."

Marshall sat down.

You Are Not Married.
But You Are Together

■ ■ ■

We met Bayram Ünlü on the European side of the Bosporus. We had been silently fighting all day — I can trace it back to Julie refusing to buy condoms at the Russian flea market. Rick was sending her some. It was early evening. We were resting near a fountain between the Blue Mosque and the Aya Sofya. Julie said, Istanbul is the quietest city we've been in.

The fountain was off. Floodlights sat in the water. There were pansies near the water and a few bushes were trimmed so that you couldn't hide behind one. Boys and men carried shoeshine boxes around their necks looking for leather. There were thousands of American students traipsing through the Sultanhamet, carrying bright packs and orange travel guides. It pained me to see new lovers. A few sat on benches opposite us consulting maps or Poste Restante mail from the Hilton helicopter. The war in the east was over and Spring Break brochures were hyping Turkey as a must-see. It was sickening to hear an American accent after a year of Turkish.

Bayram asked to join us on our bench.

I am wanting to learn English comprehension.

The accent a mixture of British and Texan. There was a

kindness in his face and Julie and I needed something
between us.

Forgive me but you are British?

Julie is, but I am Canadian. We teach English in Ankara. A
private school for the children of government officials. Bayram
seemed mildly surprised to hear of these schools.

I work for the army, he said. The air force — a radar con-
troller. Air surveillance. One of eight in Istanbul. We practice
defensive maneuvers. Against aerial attack.

I have a photo of Bayram Ünlü. Holding hands with his
daughter and Julie. The ground is flat with the low blur of a
pine forest in the distance. Julie an inch taller than him.
Bayram is stout, powerful, like a wrestler in streetclothes.
Unlike most western Turks who wear casual dark suits, no
tie, and shoes, Bayram is dressed in jeans, runners and a
beige windbreaker. His daughter, Afet, wears a red raincoat.
A plastic juice container in the shape of a radio hangs from
her neck. To the right, out of the photo, is the apartment
building Bayram and his family live in. At the time I thought
the apartments were ugly and I intentionally aligned Bayram,
Julie and Afet against the neutral background. Now I wish I
had the building. It is the last picture I have of Julie.

We met in the capital. Julie had been teaching at the Ankara
Junior Institute for eight months. The first time I met her she
said, I cannot imagine living in a city of less than four million.
We had been drinking with Glenn and Paul. I lay my feet on
the couch and Julie began massaging them. She knew I was
from Canada. Glenn and Paul were English and I was replac-
ing Rick, a Welshman who'd taken off at Christmas to thrash
olives in Crete. Julie had come to Turkey with Rick.

Glenn was a good help in finding an apartment and
showing me what absolutely had to be done to keep your

job. They drank raki and complained bitterly about teachers' salaries in Britain.

I can live on a wage of seventy pounds a month and live better than I can in London.

There'll be shoeshiners in Piccadilly, you mark my words.

When Rick left, Julie had gone with Glenn, then Paul, and it was assumed by them that I'd be next. Glenn warned me not to take it as a personal thing. When it happened I tried not to and it went well for a while. But I couldn't keep the distance. I felt invaded.

On our holidays we traveled, visiting the major Turkish cities. The Hittite ruins and fairy chimneys and Roman amphitheaters and biblical carp. We went east to Mount Ararat. We'd heard a man with a mattock near the bus depot hacking the horns off severed heads of cattle. The chopping of the bone echoing off the mountain.

Rick kept her supplied with good quality condoms. They held an uncomplicated attitude towards sex, an open relationship.

You've got to do more if you want to keep a woman, Julie said to me, as if I could keep her. My fingers weren't light enough. I was selfish in bed.

It's you I'm selfish about. I want all of you here.

But her head held Rick. He wrote her. In the last letter he'd met up with this Swiss with a stud in her nostril who'd just left her boyfriend, a Hare Krishna, and she was making a pilgrimage to the birthplace of Zeus. A Greek drove them into the mountains, then they hiked for a day past the snowline to the Dikde Cave. In the cave they could pick out a protuberance in the rock. The Greek showed them the red stone where Zeus had lain. They'd forgotten to bring a torch and used up three boxes of matches, burning their numbed fingers.

In his letters Rick wrote lists, for instance, There's three rules to follow when you thrash olives:

(1) always strike branches with a glancing blow;

(2) don't break any branches when you're climbing the tree;

(3) don't tread on any olives when they're on the nets.

He made the rules sound transferable to general conduct. Be indirect. Live without disturbing. Return without wrecking what you have left behind.

Bayram offered to show us the city. We can see the Grand Bazaar. Or visit the Aya Sofya.

Julie: Mosques are like big empty cathedrals with a pervasive odor of warm socks.

I said we'd already seen the sights.

Then I invite you home.

You live near?

It is far. He couldn't lie. I mean you will stay tonight.

We're in a hotel. We've paid already.

Which hotel?

Otel Stop.

Yes, I know the manager. I will arrange it.

We don't know you. I spread my arms knowingly.

I am not a carpet seller. My family is from a village near Izmir. If you have any clothes to wash.

We had found a bed in Otel Stop. The man in the lobby was Moroccan. He was walking across the floor on a step ladder, painting the ceiling. Julie said, He calls his country Fas, but we call it Morocco. Why can't we call it Fas?

The room small, a double bed with a sink, a chair, and blistering wallpaper. Julie checked the strength of the lightbulb. We ate around the corner at a lokanta that attempted an English menu: Greed meat rools, lamp roast, wedding soup, meat in gobbets. The food twice as expensive and half as good as food anywhere else in Turkey. They tried to charge you for the bread and no one offered a glass of tea after your meal. A boy swept cigarette ash from the tables into a funneled piece of newspaper. A man poured wooden barrels of water into a silver tank. There was a TV promoting an American car-chase. A framed poster of Mustafa Kemal Atatürk stood above the television.

We walked through the courtyard of the Blue Mosque which is very beautiful in the dark with the moon over a shoulder and the lamps highlighting minarets. It was nice because we hadn't seen it before. Julie said she'd seen the pyramids with Rick and felt disappointment. She was robbed of awe by movies, postcards, and magazine ads using pyramids as a selling prop. The spectacle was tarnished by the busloads of Americans parked by Cheops' tomb. She said they'd almost not gone.

We were in Cairo eight days and we couldn't bring ourselves to go see them. It's as if you get so close to something you've always wanted and then you lose interest. Or it changes. We couldn't lift our heads to look. We had to force ourselves to get a bus to Giza. And then we got off too early. We saw them from a distance and of course they look so big you think you're near them.

They had to walk for two hours along this road lined with hotels, bushes clipped into pyramid shapes.

From Otel Stop you can see part of one spire of the Aya Sofya. You have to look through the grated window and the steel beams of the fire escape. Julie cut three feet off the end of the grimy curtain so that it neatly covered the window yet showed the cold radiator. I said, You shouldn't do that. She held the length of the curtain, the pocketknife still locked. She said she was only modifying her environment.

It was dark as we walked to the Bosporus. Bayram bought half a kilogram of roasted chick peas. He offered the bag to us twice and said, If one man eats and another man watches, things happen. The ferry floated us down the throat of the city. The Black Sea gently pushing us into the Marmara, then the Mediterranean and eventually out to the Atlantic. You can take a ship from Odessa all the way to Canada on the slow flush of water. On the Asian side he bought a few kilograms of tomatoes, cucumbers and oranges.

My wife will not be happy with me.

A dolmus took us through thirty minutes of dark suburbs. The van with four rows of seats and they were filled. I had the laundry on my lap. Bayram handed the driver a few lira notes and tutted as we tried to pay.

We'd seen this area three days before. It had been hazy coming into Istanbul, the sun turning old on the buildings. The man across from us on the big Mercedes-Benz bus wore a flat bag of blood at his feet with a siphon snaking into his fly. An old couple in front of us were arguing. He told her to keep her coat on but she was warm she said and wanted it off. I whispered, I let you take your coat off, don't I, and Julie said, The only thing I want to know is what does a Turkish woman keep in her purse. The bus-boy worked his way up the aisle squeezing a lemon liquid into our hands. Two Americans rode in the front seats, one taking pictures of tractors hauling Singer refrigerators, the other constantly losing oranges in the aisle. As we slowed into Istanbul a bus wheel squashed a pigeon. Days later I still held the crunching, popping sound in my head.

The dolmus lumbered on. Bayram described how all people are good, nations are bad, that he preferred religious believers to atheists. He was born just after Ramadan. He said, Honesty is most important. Lies lead to truth. Truth ends in a lie. With the crush we found it hard to reply.

Bayram spoke methodically, checking each word for syntax. I take a test in May to win a place in Texas. It is a training course. Fourteen months. He will leave wife and daughter and live in a dormitory. I am committed to them, but I must learn English to understand new radar equipment.

Transistors and tubes are replaced with electronic cards. Computer instruction comes in English only.

Did you know that English is the international language of the air?

The lights of Istanbul recede. Soon we are the only passengers. Bayram leans over the front bucket seats, to instruct the driver, and we are dropped off at the edge of a field. Blocks of lit windows eight stories high stand at the far end. As we walk towards them Julie says, I guess this is where you shoot us, and Bayram says, Yes.

Latife is mad at him for not calling. He tries to curry a smile out of her. Their daughter Afet takes our hands, kisses them lightly and puts them to her forehead. She has a cold. The rooms are eleven foot square with floor tiles and rugs. Modern furniture and plants, peach walls and nine foot ceilings. There are a few photographs of Latife and Afet and the obligatory poster of Atatürk.

Bayram stacks our laundry in the washer. He is pleased with this little machine. Then he looks through his American Language booklets, circa 1964 from the U.S. Government. They are printed in English. These are my lessons. I have cassette tapes.

He plays one. A Texan reads a paragraph on the life of Paul Bunyan. The Texan repeats the paragraph, sentence by sentence, pausing long enough for the listener to repeat each line. There is a question period. The narrator asks, What kind of animal is Blue? Was Paul Bunyan a real person? The tape continues with anecdotes on George Washington Carver, porpoises and skyscrapers.

Bayram has trouble with his tee aitches. 'That this there' comes out as 'zat zis zere'. He refuses to stick tongue between teeth. It is rude to show your tongue. He does try it with a hand over his mouth and manages a perfect 'th'.

Latife had made tea and a tray with plates of cheese, tomato, cucumber, olives, and a dish of cold potato. She warms when we thank her in Turkish. The TV news. Reporters cover items in a western style. Trenchcoats and split-camera inserts.

European news is biased against Turkey. They say we treat refugees badly. Kurds. Georgians. But they are all Turkmen, why would we harm them? We get many American programs now. Soap operas even. There is a couple much like you — Denis and Cricket. We realize they are silly. No one is faithful. Simple plots. But we cannot stop watching them.

He says life is not a feeding or abating of flame. But a transformation of fire into other elements.

Julie and I help him roll out a mattress in the living room and his wife gathers extra blankets and cushions.

You are not married. But you are together.

Lying on the floor, you can see that the furniture has sheets of newspaper glued to the underside of the wood paneling. There is a picture of the Turkish president shaking hands with a western diplomat. I flick off the lamp and press into Julie. Light from other apartment windows paints the wall over the couch. We have no protection. The eyes of Atatürk pick up the light. Ice-blue eyes, contracted eyebrows.

Julie had done work for the Turkish Language Institute, translating and coining words. Atatürk, she told me, had set up the Institute in the thirties. Words like computer have to find a Turkish equivalent. Instead of *komputur* they try to get people to use *bilgisayar*, which means 'knowledge meter'. Julie said, New words have a right to live only if they bring new concepts with them. She said Atatürk read a paper by a Viennese philologist who claimed that Turkish is the mother of all languages. Atatürk liked the idea and proposed a Sun-Language Theory. As Julie puts it, Atatürk saw the birth of language when we first looked up at the sun and said "Ah!"

Our eyes adjust to the detail. Latife has left her bag on the couch.

We could look inside, Julie says.

It wouldn't be right.

She is sitting up. Her small breasts blue. I wonder where Rick is now, she says. I turn over and stare at the newspaper glued to the furniture.

Of course she catches what she has said. There's a lot of things about you, she says. But Rick. I've been open with you about Rick.

They met on a beach in Wales. Rick was living in a tent and it was September. He was suffering from two parasites he'd picked up in India. One in his small intestine, which forced him to eat only rice, lentils and a few vegetables. He refused to take antibiotics, claiming the bacteria had as much right to live as he. The other parasite lying dormant behind his left eye. Anything could trigger it to begin chewing at the optic nerve. Western medicine could offer nothing to prevent this from occurring. Julie said she admired anyone who could carry around such things.

They applied through the Turkish Embassy for the teaching positions. No photographs required. When Rick showed up in his dreadlocks they thought it was a joke. That he was wearing a wig. They wouldn't let him teach, called him

Madam-Adam, meaning transvestite. He bummed around Ankara for a few months, living with Julie, before heading to Crete.

Glenn and Paul both liked Rick. They imagined him returning to the youth hostel with olives in the cuffs of his trousers, twigs in his dreadlocks, and a pocketful of sage picked from the ridge to use in his tea. I was a Canadian who didn't even speak French. Julie liked this fact — that I was so close to being American. Living on the border. Getting their TV, their food, their pollution. She wanted to visit Arizona. See the Grand Canyon.

Latife fixes hardboiled eggs. Afet likes hers soft. Sliced cucumber, cheese, butter, tea, bread and salt. Sugar made from beets in their hometown. Their fathers are brothers. They farm together. Our laundry hanging stiff on the concrete balcony. The sun just making the angle over the apartment block east of us. Afet's cold has turned into German measles, so we cut our visit. Outside on the grass I take the photograph. I have yet to send them a copy.

A bus to the hospital and a wave goodbye. The bus filled with twice as many people standing as sitting. The ferry. Julie with pistachios from the Golden Horn. People crowding aboard. We lean over the railing, prying shells apart. If one man eats and another listens. Galata Bridge a raft floating on the water. Men take your weight for fifty lira, refill disposable lighters for a hundred. Boys with trays of pretzels on their heads. Men in caiques fry fish and sell them on chunks of bread. Silver trays of tea in ropes pulled up the sides of buildings.

Next to us at the rail stands an old man. He is staring straight ahead at the mist covering the European bank. He is leaning heavily on his crossed forearms, wearing a comfortable tweed suit and dark cape. He fingers half a cigarette nervously and he is whistling slightly through his dentures. I say, not knowing what else to say, You must be proud of your country. He stares at us as if awaking from a deep dream. I meant Europe, he says.

We've reached the west bank and the man adroitly squeezes himself into the throng. We watch him step aground then promptly turn around and melt into the flow of passengers waiting to purchase tokens for the return trip to Asia.

At Otel Stop the Moroccan has the three feet of curtain on his desk. Why did you do this? he asks. He looks hurt then angry as Julie tries to explain.

We visit the Mosaic Museum. It used to be King Constantine's Palace. The deep floors hold fans of stone patterned into saints and Süleyman. There is one of a man hiding behind a green bush. The bush turns into a beard. Unlike the chalk horses of Salisbury or Aztec landing strips, the faces can only be understood while standing on them. They only begin to disintegrate if you get close enough to kiss.

Dissolve

■ ■ ■

She had a ghostmark on her wrist from where her watch shielded the sun and her bra left dents in her shoulders where the straps dug in. And right now I'm struck with an idea for a film. The scene of lovers on a vacant street. They nuzzle noses, rub cheeks like cats. She's on the sidewalk and he's on the pavement. She absentmindedly strokes the crotch of his jeans, then cups the pouch of his sausage and eggs. Nothing else happens, just this show of affection. They walk together, not holding hands for it is too hot, but brushing shoulders. Sort of leaning into each other.

They begin humming a tune, then singing the words. At the end of each line they leave the right amount of space before resuming the song. It is important for them not to miss the space the instruments fill. They listen to their sound as one listens to music coming from another room. Overhearing it instead of confronting it directly.

I have caught up to a story of you. I have caught it, but I haven't cleaned it yet. It is fresh, stiff and red, but still raw. I have yet to put the knife to it. To thumb clean the spine and separate the head from the body. To rinse your story under cold water.

Slow dissolve. They follow a path into woods and come upon a large building. "Is it a hotel or an apartment block?" and she says, "Must be a hotel. All the curtains are the same." But there is no sign, no advertisement on the roof and some of the balconies have potted plants sunbathing.

They enter the shaded lobby and surrender their passports. Climb the stairs to the fifth floor. The wide windows in their room overlook the developing city, the twenty story scrapers with top floors propped up on peeled logs and lumber. The clouds are lighter than the sky and the sun frames the corners of highrises.

"The thing I like about being high," she says, "is you know what it's like as soon as you look. The weather's all around you. When you're low you only get bits and you can't add it up until you step outside."

They check the bed and find plastic slippers beneath it. They kiss and search for areas other than lips. They prefer shoulders and knees and nipples and collarbones. Each kiss is as cold as a chisel. As she leans over him to try a pelvis she stops. From the periphery they had mistaken the cross on a church for the cusp of a moon. Instead of falling over the horizon the white glow had stayed rigid. "May you not have to believe in God," he says. "The body of text is the body of Christ."

"Did I ever tell you," she begins, "Did I ever tell you, when I was young, I thought you shouldn't put a spoon you've licked into a jar."

She leaves one wet hipbone for another.

"It wasn't for hygienic reasons, just I thought saliva was what dissolved food. I thought if it could escape it would dissolve the world."

She turns him over, exposing a delicate line of vertebrae.

"I'd lick the spoon very carefully," she tongues each disk, moistening them like postage stamps, "to wipe off most of the saliva," she reaches his neck. "Before plunging it back in the jar."

144

She lets her breasts relax on his back.

"I always had a fear, though, that whoever opened the jar next, would find nothing in it."

Stay the Way You Are

■ ■ ■

So Sam asked God. He was climbing the stairs in the dark, asking for a sign. Sam said, in his head, God, I need to know if Martha is the one.

He opened the bedroom door. Flicked on the light. He looked at his bed and there she was — on her back, her little feet pressed out of the blankets. Her gold hair flung on the pillow. She lifts her neck, scrunches her eyes at the brightness. She is here. It hadn't occurred to Sam that she could be here, but she is and he knows it is the sign that he is looking for. But the sharpness fades and he thinks, Well, it's not that remarkable that she's here. And soon he has the sign twisted into a normal event.

He couldn't really believe in God, anyway.

Martha knew all of this.

She stared at the floor, at the walls, the table, the mattress on the floor and even the clay vase with dried flowers, searching, not for some addition, a stain or a ruffled signature of their being together, but an absence in the objects of their former selves. She wanted to see the physical appearance of things diminished since she had lain in his bed.

Why this diminished appearance?

Because she knew Sam thought she was stealing from him. She robbed him of his self. Or, taking the blame for his own

146

fate, she helped him disintegrate. He was not in control, his direction uncharted.

That was after three months. Then Martha moved in and three years passed. One night they were pulling out of the mall parking lot, about to enter the traffic steaming down Kenmount Road, when Martha said, Look.

Over to the side, in the corner of the parking lot, was a high canvas trailer. There were doors on the side of the trailer, swung open, and a man in a black suit stood at a podium bathed in a cone of light. Behind him glowed a tall gold cross. A couple dozen cars had pulled up around the trailer. The man leaned into a microphone. A slight rain fell. Sam pulled over.

When they stopped a boy trotted up, tapped on the window. Sam rolled it down. The boy placed a speaker on the window. He adjusted the volume, the knob crackling, nodded in at Sam and Martha. God and you, the boy said.

It was a drive-in evangelical service. The preacher's name was Jimmy Boland. Jimmy thanked those who joined in late and asked them to wink their high beam to let him know they were there with God's spirit. Sam went for the lights, but stopped. The mirror flashed. He turned down the volume and stared at the woman sitting next to him.

Sam and Martha are nearing thirty. They are surprised at their own intimacy, that they are, in fact, very childish. They have pet names, they use baby talk. But they've known each other, or have known of each other, since junior high. They have heard stories through mutual friends. Each living in the peripheral sphere of the other, never enough to consume or to be consumed by the other. They even grew up in the same small town, went to school together, a grade apart. They both moved to St. John's to study at Memorial. And this is a comfort. They have a common store of memory, although their impressions of the past differ greatly.

When people ask, Oh how did you meet? they are slightly embarrassed. They have no story to tell, nothing dramatic. No flash of knowing. No fast link. They have been gradual friends. Now they are confronted with, not a new lover, but a partner in the shell of someone else. They have to figure out the truth. Peel off the lacquer. Get to what it is that is them.

Jimmy Boland's voice reaches them indirectly, from other car speakers. I don't want to listen, Sam says. Tell me a story.

Martha relieves her seatbelt.

My family never talked, she says. We were pleasant to each other. We didn't fight. But there was little communication. I found love through experiences.

They let us do what we wanted. I never had to wash dishes. I mean I did, but I didn't have to. We never fought over TV shows. I was never told when to come home. I'd just say where I was going. That's why I don't think about cooking or cleaning up, or telling you I'll be late, because I never had to. It doesn't occur to me.

Do you like the woodstove?

I love the woodstove. I'm just not cracked about every weekend cutting wood. Operating a Skidoo, how much gas do we burn getting out to the woods? How much is a woodstove? Cleaning the chimney of creosote. How much is your back worth, Sam? How much your time? Running a chainsaw. Sharpening the teeth. Mixing the oil and gas. God, the racket of a chainsaw, all day long. And the fury in getting the wood. The rush, the absolute drive to get as much wood in a day. Sometimes I think all this expense can't be less than the cost of oil.

But you love the thermos at break time. Sitting on the

Skidoo seat, or on the load of birch chained to the sled. Cracking the plastic cup off the thermos. Unscrewing the plug. Vapor rising. Eating our corned beef sandwiches and hearing the trace buzz of chainsaw left hanging in the trees.

You know I love that, Sam.

Sam notices that the cars have been parked in rows. There is a corridor leading from Jimmy Boland down to where they have parked. Sam sees the preacher pointing, pointing at them.

My father, Sam says, we called him Rogie. Rogie would mark the label of the 7-Up bottle. He came home once and some was gone. No-one owned up to it. We were sent to our rooms. I said Frank, why don't you tell him. Tell Rogie you drank it, and he yelled I didn't, that's why, I didn't!

Mom and Rogie got into it. A fight about other things, food-related. It's feast or famine around here. There's no butter or margarine. My mother would spread shortening on the bread. She called it white butter and I preferred it. We drank powdered milk.

I thought of that when you were in the bathroom, dabbing your eyes and I said, Martha, you know what you are? You're a first class bitch, that's what. And I walked to the porch, shoved my arms down the sleeves of my coat. The jingle of keys. I thought, Sam, that is exactly what Rogie would do.

You went to the bedroom. I heard you in the closet. I wanted to warm up the car but you were crying. You said I can't take this anymore, this is too much. Over and over.

Martha, to hear you out of control. I crept in to you and saw you kneeling in the closet. The light showing the sleeves of my shirts. The peg with my belt. You had pulled the suitcase out of the closet. You were unpacking blue and white bags of sugar. There was a shortage in Cuba and you were stocking up. There were seven 2-kilo bags. All our sweetness lying there in seven bags. Then you opened the third drawer in the chest. Your drawer. I said Martha, you can't go, and you said Sam I love you but I can't take the pressure. I wasn't made for it. I'll have you killed.

You couldn't leave the house without me holding you. I held your hand and led you back to the seven bags of sugar. That made things right again.

Sam turns up the preacher. Jimmy Boland is pointing out over the vehicles, to some distant point past the shopping mall, some place west of where they are, as if a destination is always a little further west, a little further. His voice scratches over the monitor. Wait for the change, he says. Don't be rigid. Don't build love on a vision.

I have a scar, Martha says over Jimmy. On my finger from a spark when I was five.

She loops the steering wheel with her ring finger. Sam has never given her a ring.

A family bonfire. The spark twirled quick in the air, darted in the wind as if it was looking where to go, landed on my finger and dug in. I stared at it. My mother had to brush it off. The scar, look, it's four times larger now.

You're four times bigger.

I've had big burns that have disappeared. With some there's no reminder.

What multiplies the cells in a scar, or a mole. My moles are moving, Sam thinks. Growing. They erupt with a hard surface and then subside. The surface of my body is changing. I am no longer growing into a better body. I'm disintegrating.

Can you stay the way you are?

As they pull out of the parking lot Sam is longing for something more. He knows this is his problem. Longing is nothing but the candle flicker of thought, of an absence, a faith that cannot be sustained, which will erode into the gravel of any relationship. Love is not ignition of gasoline, but the slow turn of bone to oil. He knows this and yet he longs with a desire as large as any conversion.

Camera Obscura

■ ■ ■

Paul Harlow works at the atomic level. The tiniest living things in the universe. At supper he describes the latest experiment. He slices bacteria, placing a segment of DNA into a loop of plasmid. He uses an enzyme as a scalpel. The DNA pretends, like a virus, that it's wanted, that the plasmid needs to reproduce it.

Paul bunches his fingers like claws. He is a man who understands the pulse of electricity in the walls. How cells stick together and mitochondria make them work.

You can't see the DNA, you just have to believe that it's there.

He explains it all in such detail we could run the experiment ourselves.

We are very far removed, he says, from the things that make us work. The stethoscope? It was invented so a doctor no longer had to put his ear to the patient's chest. The length a fraction greater than the leap of a flea.

I have rented a room in this house for the past three years. The street is called — and no one knows why — Bletch. Taxi drivers sometimes think you are swearing when you give the address. There's a good crew here. An optician, Bill, who met his wife in this house: Kim's a physiotherapist. And my girlfriend Rhonda moved in — she's studying social work. I liked how Bill put it, when he and Kim decided to stay even after their marriage: you only live with other people for a short time in life. We've got the rest of our lives to live together, alone.

When Paul Harlow first phoned about a room he explained, in his English accent, that he'd seen several other places and that the price at Bletch was cheaper, although our location wasn't as handy.

I said, This is a cooperative household. We are halfway between the university and downtown, a fifteen minute walk from both.

Yes, he said, but I catch most of my own food. He explained that he fished for trout in Quidi Vidi and when the caplin run he fetches a few buckets and freezes them. I have caplin twice a week all year round, he said. I pick berries and make jam and pies. There are quite a few trees in St. John's and in winter I have a tremendous view. When there's a power failure, he said, you can look out at night and pinpoint exactly which part of the city is affected. And then in spring a sort of green haze appears and by June only half the town is visible.

So why are you moving?

Ah, he said. They are turning my wing into laboratories.

Paul came by to look. He rode his bicycle, the temperature sub-zero.

Ah, yes, he said, shaking the cold out of his shoulders. I checked the thermometer outside and I phoned the airport to get the windchill and I gathered it wasn't cold enough to freeze flesh, but perhaps I erred.

He removed his bicycle helmet. Underneath a scarf over his head and ears. He has a narrow face and a thin nose. His eyes have thick, red lids and they float out a little at the sides.

He keeps a thin moustache. We shook hands. Rhonda, Kim and Bill. A surprisingly warm hand. He noticed the avocado plant, a toaster and kettle hanging from the wall. There were two paperbacks in the toaster. A cardboard rooster head on the pelmet. Lobster claws hanging from a spider plant.

May I see the room?

He paced off the floor heel to toe, his nose dripping. It's not exactly twelve foot square, is it?

It's thirteen by eleven, I said.

Which is a square foot less, I admitted.

The dimensions caused him grief. He mumbled bed, dresser, closet, sizing them with a spread of his arms. Bill told him our last roommate didn't actually live with us. He stuck cardboard to the window. A red light and plastic trays of developing solution on a long wooden table. He would come at night to do his work.

Paul shuts the bedroom door, his hand resting on the doorknob, five of us in the room. You realize that we are now talking in camera? To talk in a sealed room.

He said he was at the dentist and had to get an x-ray to check the deterioration of his jawbone. Dr Peters placed a sponge with a frame of film in his mouth, an x-ray gun pointed at his cheek. His mouth was a camera.

We show the other rooms. Tin ceilings like wedding cake. Paul shrugs off his parka. Underneath a tweed jacket with a Red Cross pin in the lapel. Rhonda tries to joke. This is the kitchen, she says to the bathroom.

Ah, yes. He catches on and laughs politely. He touches her lightly on the shoulder.

So we had him over for supper.

Kim is interested in accents. Where exactly are you from?

Paul holds his fork, frozen. That, he says, is a rather

difficult story. You see, my father worked in the very first biochemical lab in Britain.

He rests his fork, placing an elbow on the table. He has thick forearms. He begins to stroke the fold of skin beneath his eyebrow.

Just after the war, he says, my father was stationed in Malta, where I was born. For a time he was personal physician to Lord Louis Mountbatten. But then we quickly returned to England. To Yorkshire. And then the government built a new facility just outside of Salisbury —

The higher ark, Bill says.

Rhonda interrupts to ask about his Red Cross pin. How many litres do you have to give to get one.

Fifty, he says, and then clarifies: Not all at once.

The first person he'd met on coming to Newfoundland was the President of the local Chapter of the Red Cross. He had the window next to Paul and they switched seats so Paul could see the city from above.

And do you cook?

Well yes, of course I cook. What I normally do is on Sunday I'll prepare an enormous amount of fish or spaghetti or last week it was stew. And then I'll pack them into one litre margarine tubs. I'll make six to last the week. I'll have sandwiches for lunch and the tub for supper. But I'm just thinking I couldn't possibly take up space in your fridge with all that food.

Paul wants to know how we divide the shelves. Where would he put his milk, for instance.

Rhonda explains our system of Cooking, Cleaning and Conversation. He thinks this a fine idea, cooking one meal and getting four in return. He can get used to that. However.

It's just that I never know what time I can get back. You see I'm at the lab and then on Tuesday nights there's Scottish Country dancing and on Sundays there's choir and then on alternate Wednesdays the Natural History Society has its meeting. Oh, and this Monday the annual bird count will be conducted and Thursday I have a Red Cross meeting where I take minutes, so I can't be late for that.

Rhonda says we could always leave it in the oven.

We wave at his white helmet. The rear generator light glows a weak red signal down Bletch. It's as if he can't tell what's important, Bill says. Can't edit. Doesn't know where one story starts and another ends.

It's not easy living with other people.

You see phrases of life from breakfast to bed. The rushed cups of morning coffee and the plates with peanut butter and toast crumbs. The heart expressed in pet voices. You don't have to imagine what people are like, alone. People who are not like yourself. Who have other foibles and other loves. If you live with people long enough you cannot believe that you all, in the end, hold the same values.

Paul moves in on the first of May. Bill says, I measured his eyes, and the ratio is amazing. I used my ruler — except he said, That is not a ruler. That is a scale. He has twice the average distance between his eyes. If he came to my store I'd have to get him frames custom-made.

He promises to be gone by September, and this is good, I tell him. Four months. We can plan a life with you. We know the trajectory. When to have a farewell. It's not often you live with finity.

It's my visa, he says. Stamped until September.

We speak over the rim of the blanket hooked across the kitchen entrance. I can see his head floating, the straps of his apron.

He buys the furniture he's had at Southcott Hall. He says he has grown familiar with the desk. It has the proper kneehole. There's a small brown bookcase for which he has just enough books.

But I need a bed.

In the paper we find him one that folds. He carries it to Bletch on his bicycle. I watch him set it up. He lies on the bare mattress.

It has a tendency to sag in the middle, doesn't it. If I was heavier at my feet and head, it wouldn't pose a problem.

To the top pane of the window he has taped a blue chest x-ray. He says it is his chest. He had to have it for immigration.

I tell him I have never seen a real x-ray. He says that lungs are not like balloons, but more like broccoli. The black triangles of the lungs cast a shadow over his shirt.

Four months pass this way. For instance, the nights. Paul absolutely must devote some time each night to bettering himself.

There are three things: I have to catch up on my letter-writing. There's some scientific literature. And I must go out to meet women.

It's all right, he says, for us to stay in, because we all have someone.

But I haven't had a hug on this side of the Atlantic. People are friendly, but they're not much for hugs.

Rhonda says today she locked the door because she was the only one home. Paul arrived a minute later. Gracious, Rhonda, this is not America. You don't have to lock the door.

She'd said, There are derelicts living in the basement next door. I've been attacked in this city, and an ex-convict I've worked with knows that I live in this house. He was sorry then. He said he hadn't thought of all those conditions.

The weekends. Often he rides to Brigus South to spend them with Ivan and Sandra. I've heard about Sandra. She works in Paul's lab at the university. She once kept a hawk, but it killed all her doves, so she shot the hawk and ate it. Ivan built the house using limbed trees still rooted as a framework. The walls follow the path of the trees. They haven't a phone so Paul has no way of inviting himself down. He just appears.

It takes me four hours to pedal there, he says. It's usually nighttime and I've discovered how winding the road is. By day you don't notice. But at night the constellations turn completely around, so actually you're heading north instead of south.

Before leaving Bletch he checks the weather. He opens the front door and, with hands held behind his back, strolls a few yards across the walk, into the road, checking the heavens from right to left, wheeling and returning to the porch.

We get used to Paul carrying his shortwave radio from room to room. The ebbing whine of BBC, the antenna up. He talks to it. He says, Good, glad to hear it. He says the BBC has excellent continuity. He makes sandwiches from tinned meat and sliced bread, cut into triangles. In a tupperware box with an apple, a muffin. Carries it to work in his left pannier. He'll come home late and eat leftovers hunched over the speaker. When I'm in Rhonda's room I hear him listening at low volume, shivering in the cold.

Kim heard him one morning, trying to jump out of bed to put the garbage out. Paul was on garbage and he'd heard the truck approaching, halting, starting up again. The tiny, short moans coming from his room. Is he masturbating?

I've only had three hours sleep, he told her. He lay crumpled in his bed for twenty minutes massaging the muscles in his legs. Complete agony.

Kim worked the muscles free. Paul said You are such a good kinesiologist. It's those back exercises, she said. That bar clamped to your door frame. He grips the bar, pulls his legs through, and dangles from his knees upside down. You can think you're alone, walk up the stairs, and get confronted with this bat silhouette, the sun streaming past him. Quietly hanging there. It straightens my vertebrae, he says, swaying, arms dangling like thin leather wings.

Trout tonight. At least that is the promise. However the freezer at the lab has been tampered with. Paul discovered it packed with three to five pound fish.

Salmonids of some description.

He unpacked all the fish. But the trout were gone.

All I found was a package of my frozen caplin. Then I tried putting the salmonids back — and they'd been put in so tightly that it was very difficult to get them all in. I had two or three left over with it jammed tight and I didn't want to leave the lid open and the fish tails were starting to droop. I asked Sandra but she knew nothing. I can't think of what they've done with my trout.

Bill says that perhaps they've thrown them out.

I mean they're trout. Who wants a fridge full of trout?

Paul is reduced to the caplin. He retrieves from his saddlebag a package with 2lb 4oz marked on the side. He has a set of scales for weighing fish, berries, mushrooms and airmail letters.

It takes Paul six and a half minutes to clean and dry one caplin. He squeezes each one in a cheesecloth he keeps folded in a box in his room. He eyes his watch on the counter.

At dinner Paul frowns at the way Bill is flaking the meat from the bones.

Fish have a lateral line, he explains. You guide your knife along it to peel away the meat.

He scrapes his plate clean with the blade of his knife, making a line of horizontal marks on the surface. Bill asks if all his family does that.

Only my grandfather, I am told. I never knew him.

So it's genetic.

Yes. It may be.

When Paul washes the dishes he opens the cupboard doors below the sink, so he can bend his knees.

In August Paul is granted an extension from Immigration. Although he must get home for Christmas.

I've been away for five of them.

One hand is grasping a folded newspaper. His tie tucked in after the second button.

My mother has just sent this.

Of small circulation and fourteen years old, the newspaper has all three male Harlows in it.

The front page his father, Dr Peter Harlow. The photograph stern and grave. The column on the effects of a certain chemical on civilian populations.

The Arts section, Paul's brother Teddy with an arm raised. A rock concert raising money for African famine. Teddy's group is occupying the upper levels of the Eiffel Tower. A guitar strap on his shoulder.

On the back page Paul. With two drawings, comparing the old train tracks in Salisbury with the new proposed line. The drawings are intricate, the vanishing points precise, the detail exquisite. There is so much detail that the differences are hard to discern. Everything is in focus. A short article notes Mr Harlow's contribution to the accurate recording of rail transportation in southwest England.

I haven't drawn much since schooldays, he says. I would win prizes at the village fête for best drawing.

Paul gets a chance to spend a week on Brunette Island, studying a buffalo and collecting fungi samples. Sandra accompanies him. The buffalo is the last of a herd introduced in the sixties.

They return holding hands, with four bags of chanterelles and shaggy manes. They are weighed, recorded and then sautéed for breakfast. The three of us eat together on the back deck. The grass is tall and the foxglove are bending under their own weight.

Sandra says That buffalo was deranged. It had come to believe it was the only buffalo left in the world.

Paul didn't take photos of the buffalo.

You see I've never had many pictures. I tend to save everything. I thought if I had a camera it would just be another box of things I'd have to find a place for or throw away. I don't have any pictures from school, which I regret now, but then I hated school. I was beaten up terribly all the time and later on it was mental torture. They'd throw the shoe brush at me as I fell asleep. When school pictures were done I never bought them. I refused. During the Arctic expedition my mother asked me to get someone to take a picture of me, just so she would have a record of my time there.

Sandra. Yes, Sandra. Attractive, dark hair. A little short. Her own car, a vw. She talked about tree rings and calcium deposits. She was raised a Hindu, but she's white. She touched Paul in a very close way.

Amazing.

What about Ivan?

Well he's crushed. She told him the house is his. His trees. You'll see her tonight. They're cooking squid.

MICHAEL WINTER

Rhonda said you can only know sides of people. We are blind to the wedges we leave open.

It's easy to clean, Sandra explains. The squid is a leftover from the lab.

You separate the mesentery from the body: it's fascinating what things hold us together, isn't it? No stone left unturned. Every possibility tried.

When she's gone I explain to Paul that there's no problem in having a guest over. For the night.

Ah, yes, he says. Perhaps I will make use of that.

After supper we read Primo Levi's memoirs. It's Bill's book. It has photographs of the death camps. Models of the underground showers where they gassed the prisoners. Paul and Sandra scrutinize the photos. They think the pictures of the chambers are a bit unrealistic.

The prisoners couldn't possibly be crammed in six-deep.

Bill says, Photos don't lie.

Paul replies that it is only a model.

Bill: Are you doubting their existence?

Their voices rise over each other. Paul is adamant. They've exaggerated. Condensed the space. Bill: Conditions were extreme. The guards packed them in.

Paul abruptly swings his hand up near Bill's nose, to show the proximity. And Bill, instinctively, draws back to hit him.

Rhonda points out that the photos lack depth, that Paul is looking at the bodies in the distance as if they are on top of the ones in front.

I see.

She adds that there are people who have gone blind after seeing atrocities done to their families. There's nothing wrong with their vision, but they can't see. The brain has switched off the horror.

Yes, he says again. I understand.

He worked in Mursden Hospital, just on the periphery of London. From his window he could see seventeen miles straight across the rooftops to St. Paul's Cathedral. And from the verandah on the opposite side stretched acres of green pasture.

When he first went there he got sick and was a patient on his own ward. It gave him respect for his patients, the work of the nurses and staff.

A woman who had a wasting disease was put on his ward. The muscles in her throat wouldn't swallow, so saliva would build up and she couldn't eat. As they were coaxing a tube down her throat the vagus nerve was alerted. The nerve runs from the brain to the esophagus. It's the tenth pair of nerves running from the brain — the only one not to be connected through the spinal cord, but directly from the brain to the esophagus and the heart.

It was a freak occurrence, but the nerve was triggered. It sent a message to the heart to stop pumping. The woman went into cardiac arrest. The ward nurse asked if they should start the heart again and Paul said no. Let her go. She's going anyway, let her go this way. Relatively painless.

The husband was very upset when Paul told him. Paul didn't mention that he could have revived her.

To change the topic Bill sings a song about Kegan whose wife is a seal in disguise. Bill can haul chords out of the air. The toaster buzzing is a B. The kettle whistle is a high C. In the end the woman returns to her natural form to fetch his wrecked dory from a storm. She lies beside Kegan, protecting him from the cold, and they die with the snow gently covering them. Bill holds one hand over the other as they perish.

On Thanksgiving Sandra drops by. We haven't heard her and Bill is saying it's all or nothing with Paul. His focus is both microscopic and telescopic. The middle range eludes him. Then we see her in the porch, dark against the light.

She's driving Paul to supper. No, she won't come in. I watch her sitting in the VW, reading. In the field the dogberries are orange. The leaves are torn off and there's wind on the branches. Kids playing pennant ball. I ask Rhonda what she thinks. She says Paul is probably telling her things.

Telling her what?

Stories about us.

What kind of stories.

Whatever stories he has. He has stories.

But at 5:05 he arrives.

Yes, Sandra.

He rushes upstairs, halts halfway, and keeps saying aloud, Fascinating. Yes, quite.

He descends, bicycle helmet still on, and says, Do you know what a camera obscura is? and then, Would you like to see one?

I follow him on the stairs. He points to the dark wallboard on the landing. A small disk of light burns, with a square of opaque light surrounding it. I get Rhonda off the phone. I tell Kim and Bill they should come look at this. I hesitate at the front door.

Her window is open. I explain what is occurring inside.

You know, she says, I want you to know something. Sandra steps from the car. That's obsession in there. I want you to know I'm with an obsession and that is rare.

She says when she first saw Paul it was at a distance. He was standing by the road and he was touching a star. Then he leaned over the star, climbed it, and guided it towards her.

Then she saw that the star was a bicycle, glinting in the sun.

We open the door to a black house.

That light, Paul explains, is coming through the keyhole in my bedroom door. That is the sun. This is the chimney inverted and that's the roof of the house opposite. That's the telegraph pole.

We watch as the sun sinks at an angle. On the wallboard it rises. We see smoke from a chimney pass over the sun. Birds fly upside down. Bill: the wall is like a retina. We're lucky it's exactly this distance, that everything is in focus.

The show lasts twenty minutes. The sun rising behind some trees. We have passed that light a hundred times without noticing it. We watch the sun arc over the wood grain. The upside down chimney. There is a blurry patch we can't decipher. Then Paul realizes it must be his chest x-ray in the window. Yes, that is my lung, there, upside down.

We can pick out ribs, a clavicle.

Sandra says she's had curtains with cigarette burns. The sun in the morning appearing on the wall in several places.

We watch until the last of the light fades off the wallboard. Kim says we should have made popcorn.

Snow arrives on Hallowe'en. It drifts up Bletch like a ghost. The kids don't seem to like our street, so we're left with a bowl of brown candy and suckers the colour of traffic lights.

Paul is on to noble gases. He's sent a tag list to an international genetic consulting body.

I still won't know exactly what it is, he says, but I can get a picture of its evolution and place.

He and Sandra have been placing a mass of DNA in a castellated gel sandwiched between glass plates. An electric current pulls injected proteins through the gel. They are excited by this. Bigger molecules go slower than smaller ones. A dye traces their path. The dye contains a radiation with a halflife of 87 days. X-ray crystallography picks up the luminous trail.

It's late night. Paul explains that he can't work during the day. There are too many distractions.

I've decided to alter my sleep cycle.

He'll work at night and go to bed at breakfast. Every night until he goes. Paul looks intently at the TV.

I have never seen this program. I have heard it through a wall from another apartment.

Spock and Kirk are beaming down to an alien city. This interests Paul. He is convinced that humans will leave Earth and populate other planets. He explains that, because of the immense distances, we will develop into separate species. The earth is middleaged. In another five billion years the sun will turn into a Red Giant and consume us. This era of progression is our only chance to take life off Earth.

We'll never communicate fruitfully with other lifeforms because a message will take so long to travel, he says, his arms far apart. There'll be no way for one group to control another. No threat. People will behave as if life did not exist elsewhere, because it won't matter to them.

Rhonda says she hates the show because there are no trees.

In December Paul gives his notice. We put up new signs. He's rushing to finish work, to pack, to get a cheap ticket. Sandra tries to drive him but he says he misses his bike. They look at each other furtively, afraid of his departure. Each day, we think, may be it. We see him in the morning going to bed and then rising at supper for breakfast. He is bicycling in windchill factors of minus twenty. It begins with a cough. A ragged breath. Then his chest is sore. Sandra diagnoses microplasma pneumonia. He will take anthromysen for ten days.

Paul's mother calls. She says, Tell him this is long distance. But he's not up. She thinks she has the time zones wrong. I want to tell her the wrong hour. She is very concerned to get the message down in under one minute. It's about Spain, his brother, and Christmas.

When he wakes Paul reads the note aloud. He shuffles through his cardboard boxes, taking one to the living room. He starts hauling out lengths of artificial tree. Bill says, Paul, there's three weeks to Christmas. And we usually get a real one. Paul: You mean you won't be going home?

Bill: Bletch is home.

I meant your parents'.

I don't have any parents, Paul.

Ah. You're all staying?

We are.

He pauses, then says It's difficult getting a cheap flight. It's all booked until the new year. In fact, my mother would prefer if I returned in February, or the spring even. My brother plans to visit Salisbury in the spring.

The visa, if he changes it to a visitor's permit, would last until then.

We can be a little family here, he says. And at least look at it first.

A Scotch pine. The needles are the plastic in green garbage bags. He says he's had it several years, but never a chance to put it up. I've housesat on previous Christmases and they've always had a tree.

We take a vote: a real tree. We set a time for noon Sunday.

Paul: But I have choir then.

Well Rhonda works at five.

I see. I could go to Evensong, I suppose. But there's a lunar eclipse on Sunday. Oh, alright.

But on Sunday his bike is gone. The tires imprinting the snow like garden hose.

We drive out the highway. We choose an ugly tree. The trunk is bent, branches are missing along one side. Some of the needles are red. Kim says, It's perfect. Bill says, Paul's not going. He'll never go. He'll get Sandra pregnant and they'll move in to that little room forever.

At Bletch the bike is back. Snow melting from the rims. Paul's tree is packed in the box by the stairs. A faint whine of shortwave ebbs over the kitchen blanket. We can see the shadow of their embrace upon it.

Bill says, So you changed your mind.

Paul's head appears at the rim of the blanket. He has the apron on over his coat. He explains that he hadn't made up his mind to go. There was the moon to think of. It was his turn to say the prayers at church and there were those flood victims in Pakistan.

But it was either me or Rhonda, and I understand you going in the afternoon.

He studies the tree, but doesn't come in to trim. He says, If it's all right, Sandra and I would like to make some mincemeat pies. They are watching the moon from the kitchen window. In the backyard there is a shadow of the roof and the chimney, smoking on the snow. We join them when the earth finally obliterates the moon.

On the stairs his open door, the bedroom window. The x-ray and the moon. I want to see the moon as the earth's shadow leaves it, illuminating his chest.